The

O Paddy dear, and did you hear the news that's going round?
The shamrock is forbid by law to grow on Irish ground;
I met with Napper Tandy and he took me by the hand,
And he said, "How's poor ould Ireland, and how does she stand?"
She's the most distressful country that ever yet was seen;
They're hanging men and women there for the wearing of the green.

Popular ballad

The
Wearing of the
Green

LINDA NEWBERY

Lions
An Imprint of HarperCollinsPublishers

First published in Lions 1992

Lions is an imprint of the Children's Division,
part of HarperCollins Publishers Ltd,
77-85 Fulham Palace Road, Hammersmith, London W6 8JB

Printed and bound in Great Britain
by HarperCollins Manufacturing Glasgow

Contents

Acknowledgements

I would like to acknowledge my debt to the authors of the books I have found most useful as background reading for *The Wearing of the Green*.

Vera Brittain's *Testament of Youth* and Lyn Macdonald's *The Roses of No Man's Land* have been invaluable and fascinating reading in preparation for this and my two other novels set during the First World War.

John Masefield's *Gallipoli*, first published in 1916, describes the Dardanelles campaign in detail and gives an evocative sense of the terrain.

Robert Kee's excellent and absorbing historical trilogy *The Green Flag* helped me to understand Irish affairs of the time. Ruth Dudley Edwards' *Patrick Pearse: The Triumph of Failure* gave insights into the personality of a man whose credentials as saint or madman are still disputed in Ireland and beyond. Peter de Rosa's *Rebels*, which chronicles events before and during the Rising in meticulous detail, was immensely useful, as were *Dublin 1916* edited by Roger McHugh and *1916: The Easter Rising* edited by Owen Dudley Edwards and Fergus Pyle, both of which give a range of opinions and viewpoints.

My motivation for writing the book is, I suppose, best summed up by the Irish saying: Ireland's history is something the English should remember and the Irish should forget.

PART ONE

MEDITERRANEAN,
1915

Surfacing

Coming back to consciousness was like floating slowly up to the surface of a dark lake. When the smarting of his eyes told him he had reached daylight, he lay as exhausted as a hooked fish snatched out of its proper element. But he was alive and breathing, a notion which his mind could only register with dim, detached curiosity.

At last he opened his eyes and stared upwards in puzzlement at a white ceiling which seemed to rotate drunkenly. A wave of nausea rose to his throat and he closed his eyes until he felt sure that he was lying stably on a horizontal surface, in no danger of being tipped off. His ears, dutifully performing their normal functions, were filtering background noises: a woman's voice speaking cheerfully, a metallic clatter, and a meaningless continuous mumbling and groaning which seemed to be coming from someone a few yards away. He opened his eyes again and craned his neck far enough to see that he was lying in a bed. His body was covered with a grey blanket, and there was a row of identical beds, all with hunched shapes prone or propped in them, and pale-clad figures moving about from one to another.

He tried to sit up to see better. Fire seared across his stomach like a branding-iron, and he fell back against the pillow, muffling his face into it to stop himself from shouting out loud while the talons of pain flamed and probed and gouged at his intestines. He could only clench his teeth and try to ride it out, while somewhere at the edge of his mind was the knowledge that this pain was not new.

"Can you hear me?" The voice floated towards him across a black unchartable distance, but his eyelids parted reluctantly and he saw a pale female figure standing quite close. "Can you hear me?" she asked again, bending down, so that her face seemed to swim towards him. He closed his eyes, unable to speak, and heard the brisk tread of her shoes as she walked away. He felt sick with pain and confusion, trapped in his suddenly unfamiliar body.

Voices again, two women this time, in rapid hushed conversation. Then he felt strong hands grip his shoulders from behind and the slow dull pain of a needle sinking into his arm. Someone raised his head and a firm hand grasped his chin and prised open his mouth. He felt the smooth edge of a glass against his lips, and the cool trickle of water. He coughed and swallowed, and then drank some more.

The woman nodded approvingly. and said, "Good. You'll sleep now." He was lowered to the pillow and soon the lapping waves of sleep washed him away from his pain-racked body into the welcoming pool of darkness.

He dreamed that he was in some stifling, stinking place, dark, his body crammed against others. The dark air stank of sweat, urine, pus, of every kind of human excretion, with a tang of something else hot and acrid, goat-like. A voice near him was raised in a continuous wail of pain, like a cat caught in a snare. He could hardly breathe, the stagnant air cloying in his lungs, sickening him, polluting his body with its foulness. And when he tried to shift his position, the explosion of pain in his abdomen made him clench every muscle rigid. He must be half-way to hell, in some fetid Underworld for the half-dead . . .

When he next awoke, the light in the room was brighter and he could hear men talking in the adjoining beds. The air in the room smelled of disinfectant and stale sweat and smoke. Cautiously, he took stock of his physical condition. The pain in his abdomen was still there, but as an almost-tolerable background ache rather than the savage assault it had been at first. He lifted the edge of the blankets and saw that the lower part of his body was completely wrapped in thick bandages, from which two opaque tubes emerged and drooped over the side of the bed. He dropped the blanket quickly and frowned at the frayed edge, trying to recapture the fragment of memory that had nagged at him earlier.

"Be fun when they change that lot." The man in the next bed was propped up on one elbow, looking at him with bored interest. "You were in a right state last night till they gave you the morphia. Feel better now?"

He nodded, focusing with difficulty on the man's face.

"You're Second Lieutenant P. Leary," the other man said. "The Sister told me. Will Dobson,

13

me." He jabbed a thumb at his pyjama-clad chest. "What's the P. stand for?"

"Patrick." He was relieved to find that the answer came to mind so readily.

"Patrick Leary, eh? Dublin Fusiliers? You must have been lucky. There's not many of them left to tell the tale."

"No. Epping Foresters." Again the reply was automatic.

"Same as me. With a name like that I wonder you're not in an Irish regiment."

Patrick thought for a moment. "I did live in Dublin," he said slowly, "but not since I was little."

"Well, you've still got the old Oirish brogue. It's a long way from Gluepot, eh?"

"Gluepot?" Patrick repeated.

The other man looked at him quizzically. "What we were just talking about. Out there. Gluepot. Gallipoli."

Mediterranean

He was in Malta; he knew that because the man in the next bed had told him. But he couldn't remember what had happened to him.

In his waking moments, he was aware of warm air wafting in from outside, bringing with it the scent of sun-warmed thyme; billowing curtains at the windows; nurses with cheerful voices and quick efficient hands. He knew nothing of what lay beyond the small terrace he could see from the window and the pale-blue flowers which climbed luxuriantly over the balustrade. Malta: for all he could remember of arriving there, it might as well have been the South Pole.

He seemed to have become detached from his body. He could see it, and at intervals people came and did messy and disgusting things to it. For most of the time it was a heavy lump of disfigured flesh which seemed to have nothing much to do with him. From time to time it reminded him emphatically that his insides were being clawed out and eaten. And then usually the nurses would come and the needle would sink slowly into his arm and he would drift away again and leave his body lying there.

The sun shone into the room, warm on his face as he lay drowsily. Doctors and nurses came and went, standing by his bed, talking in muffled voices, carrying stretchers past. Screens went up round the bed opposite, and when they were taken away again the bed was stripped bare.

Voices talked, close to him.

"No improvement . . . not responding to the irrigations . . ."

"We'll have to operate again . . ."

When he was next aware of being fully conscious, he found that he was somewhere different altogether. He was in a room with white-painted walls, no windows or sunshine or flowery scents. He raised his head cautiously. Opposite his bed ran a thick double row of pipes, and he could hear a continuous deep whirring or thrumming, which he thought at first was inside his head until he located its source somewhere beneath him. The room contained a dozen or so other beds.

He remembered that he had had a second operation. His body was constricted, but pain-free. He felt carefully under the bedclothes and his hands encountered a stiff padding of bandages. There was no sensation. It was as if he were mummified, he thought.

"Welcome back to the land of the living," a voice said.

He turned his head and saw that the person sitting up in the next bed was the man who had spoken to him before.

"Are we still in Malta?"

"No, mate. On our way back. Somewhere out in the Mediterranean."

"On a ship?"

The man grinned. "Well, stands to reason on a ship. What else?"

Patrick didn't answer. He lay back and stared at the ceiling, trying to sort out his nagging half-memories . . .

"Most of the others are in the luxury pas-senger accommodation. Trust our luck to end up in some sort of boiler-room," the voice went on . . .

. . . He had been on a ship before . . . recently . . . that dark stinking place of his dreams. But he could remember no more, and the voice that sounded in his head came from somewhere else entirely. Medi-terranean. The middle of the earth.

"It comes from the Latin, of course, *medius* and *terra*. Medi-terranean. The middle of the earth." Dr Chivers jabbed with his stick at the irregular blue shape on the scroll-map which he had pulled down over the blackboard. He moved his pointer to one of the coloured jigsaw-fragments which bordered the sea. "And this, Collard, you will have no trouble in identifying as . . . ?"

Patrick heard the boy behind him whisper the answer across the aisle, and Collard repeated it confidently. "Algeria."

Dr Chivers was not deceived. "Thank you, Peters," he said crisply to the collaborator. "Since you're clearly so eager to air your geographical knowledge, perhaps you'll identify this country . . . here." The stick wavered over central Europe for a moment before veering sharply to the south-east and landing on the large sprawling area whose profile always reminded Patrick of a grinning open-mouthed dog about to swallow the island of Cyprus.

Peters hesitated and then said, "Persia, sir."

"Think again, Peters. Our Saviour did not, unless I'm badly mistaken, use a Persian carpet for transport around the Holy Land."

There was a ripple of dutiful laughter from the twenty boys in the class. Peters corrected himself. "I meant the Turkish Empire, sir."

"Correct. And this? Leary?"

"Servia, sir."

"Good." Dr Chivers looked mildly surprised. Patrick, having answered his question, relaxed slightly on his hard seat, knowing that the interrogation would progress all the way round the class before he would be called on to respond again. He liked maps and had learned all the countries of Europe from an atlas at home long ago. He liked the strange, exotic-sounding names of foreign cities: Thessalonika, Sofia, Constantinople, Kiev. Once, when his cousin Brendan had asked him where he would most like to go in all the world, he had said Vladivostok, just because he liked saying the name.

While he listened to Blackburn Minor confusing Rumania and Bulgaria, he played his own private game of finding pictures in the countries. South America (out of sight at present on the world map rolled up at the top of the blackboard) was a spaniel with drooping ears; Italy, of course, a high-heeled cavalier's boot poised to kick Sicily, a misshapen football, smack through the Straits of Gibraltar; and his favourite, newly-discovered, the Irish Sea was a dinosaur-like monster, with an eye, the Isle of Man, and one arm reaching up the Bristol Channel as if to tickle the belly of England. It was cheating in a way; the countries were supposed to be the picture, not the sea in between, but nevertheless the monster was clearly there, a rather cheerful-looking blue monster between the pink of England and Wales and the pink of Ireland. There were lots of pink bits on the world map, and Patrick knew that they were the British Empire. Brendan said that one day Ireland would be an independent country, when the British government finally gave in; Patrick supposed that when that happened it would be given a different colour on the map, a colour of its own. But Uncle James talked about Home Rule, which wasn't quite the same thing, and would, as far as Patrick understood it, leave Ireland still pink.

Patrick, in his first term at school in England, felt very conscious of his Irishness. He hadn't realised until he came to school that he had an accent which marked him out from the other boys; he didn't say much at first, daunted by the confident English boys in his dormitory with their clipped, shrill voices. Collard, the form captain, had lost little time in drawing Patrick's oddness to everyone's attention.

"Sure if he isn't named Paddy," he told the others after lights-out. "Paddy from Dobblan, begorrah, come over to learn to read and write."

The name stuck, and he quickly learned to put up with taunts from Collard and his friends: "No use asking Paddy, he can't read," or, at meal-times, "Don't give Paddy any meat – he's only used to potatoes." In fact, he had been relieved to find that he was well able to keep up in lessons, and was even ahead in some subjects. He kept this to himself, not wanting to attract further attention from Collard.

The bell signalled the end of the lesson. "Don't let cricket this afternoon put tomorrow's test out of your minds," Dr Chivers said. "I expect everyone to get at least seventy-five percent – yes, even you, Peters. I suggest that you spend this evening's prep period in solid revision."

The class was dismissed, and Patrick put his books away, thinking without much pleasure of the afternoon in store. He usually liked sport, but he had never played cricket until coming to England. No-one had explained the rules to him, so that he had no idea what to do when told to field in the slips or go back to the crease. Some of his classmates took his hesitation as evidence of stupidity, which annoyed him. And from his limited acquaintance with cricket he took it to be a slow, boring game, involving hours of standing in the outfield or sitting by the pavilion waiting to bat. The other boys seemed to have been reared on it, wielding their own willow bats and talking knowledgeably about the County team and the advantages of various fielding positions. It seemed to be more than just a game. Skill at cricket seemed to Patrick to be a passport to social acceptance, and one which he did not possess.

After lunch, thinking that he would take his sketch-book out to the sports field, he went to retrieve it from his classroom desk. The broad corridor, smelling of polish, was barred with bright patches of sunlight from the windows which looked over the quad; no-one was around apart from Matron's ginger cat which sat washing its paws on a windowsill, and Patrick wondered whether there were some rule forbidding entry during the midday break. With this in mind, he walked quietly, and it was only as he approached the door to the form-room that he heard whispers and giggles from inside. The boys standing by the blackboard broke apart furtively as he approached, and then relaxed as they recognised him.

Collard, who was holding a stick of chalk, flushed slightly as he faced Patrick. "Just leaving a message on your behalf," he said. "We thought you'd appreciate it."

His conspirators giggled. Patrick looked from Collard's face to the scroll-map which Dr Chivers had left clipped down. In huge letters, over Ireland and across part of the Atlantic, Collard had scrawled HOME RULE FOR IRELAND.

Patrick stared. "Are you mad? You'd better clean that off before Dr Chivers sees it."

"On the contrary. I'm just about to sign your initials so that he knows who did it." Collard turned back to the map, raising his arm to write. Patrick made a grab for the chalk which Collard deftly forestalled by ducking and twisting nimbly away. In the skirmish that followed, joined by Peters and Marshall, Patrick was so intent on prising the chalk from Collard's grip that he was unaware of the heavy footsteps in the corridor until a voice snapped, "What's going on here?"

He turned guiltily, the chalk in his hand at last. The teacher was one he didn't recognise, a bespectacled grey-haired man in the black academic gown worn by all the staff, which Patrick thought made them look like enormous bats flapping their way around the corridors.

Peters spoke first. "We came in to tidy up for Dr Chivers, sir, and found Leary writing on the map. We were trying to stop him."

"That's not –" Patrick's voice was high with indignation, but the teacher silenced him with a glare and a raised finger.

"Wait until you're asked, boy. What's your name?"

"Leary, sir."

"And what have you got to say for yourself, Leary?"

"I didn't do it, sir."

"You didn't do it? You've got the chalk in your hand, boy!"

Patrick, about to protest, saw the light in Collard's eye and thought better of it. He knew the unwritten code well enough. The others had the safety of numbers on their side. He could tell the truth and pay the penalty later, or stay silent and take the blame now. He said no more, deciding that punishment inflicted by Collard and his friends would be more exacting than anything the teacher could hand out.

The teacher waited a few moments and then said, "Well then, Leary, since you've got nothing to say for yourself, I can only assume that you're responsible. I think you'd better see me this afternoon instead of going out to play cricket. I'm sure I shall be able to find some useful way of occupying you."

Later, sitting in the silent classroom looking out at the quad with its splash of yellow forsythia and smooth expanse of carefully-tended grass, Patrick thought that he hadn't got such a bad deal after all. New to boarding-school, he still felt oppressed

22

by the lack of privacy; wherever he went, there was someone telling him to hurry up, to stop running, to be quiet, to speak up. He would get the measure of cricket soon, he decided, but now the three hours of solitude stretched out welcomely. His copy of Virgil lay open in front of him, but before he started he took his sketch-book out of his desk and quickly drew a large and tubby Trojan horse, which was turning its head with ears pricked and an expression of good-humoured surprise as a door in its side opened and armed men tumbled out.

He was pleased with the picture. It was rather a pity that there was no-one here to admire it; even Dr Prowse, the history master, might approve. He tore the page out and propped it on the front of the desk before starting on the Virgil, with its tales of sea-voyages and warriors and enchanted islands. He dipped his pen into the ink-well and wrote carefully: *Arma virumque cano, Troiae qui primus ab oris Italiam fato profugus Laviniaque venit . . .*

"You were lucky to get away with that," the Medical Officer said, straightening up. "A bit further one way or the other, and you'd never have survived the internal bleeding. Nasty enough, though."

Patrick was hardly able to speak for relief that the four-hourly ordeal of having his dressing changed was over. It took all his concentration not to cry out, and the effort squeezed tears from the corners of his eyes. Three and a half hours to rest now until the next treatment. Three and a half hours to try not to think about it.

The M.O. was replacing his instruments on a tray

held by the nurse. "How far did you get, exactly?" he asked. "Most of the men here say they didn't get beyond the beach, if that far."

Patrick shook his head slowly. "I can't remember anything about it at all."

Now, God be thanked

"Shell-shock, they call it. You must be shell-shocked," Will Dobson said. "At least you haven't gone completely off your chump. Mate of mine saw a chap out at Mons who couldn't even remember his own name, nor where he came from, nothing. You're not in that state."

"No," Patrick said drowsily. "I can remember some things. It comes and goes."

"Perhaps the rest'll come back to you in time."

Dobson, whose injuries were not serious, was able to go up on deck from time to time, returning with weather reports and details of progress. Patrick wished he were able to see for himself. He could recall nothing at all of the outward voyage, while his mental charting of the Mediterranean – Samothrace and the Cyclades, Cythera and Carthage – brought to mind the wanderings of Aeneas and Ulysses rather than his own recent travels.

He spent most of the time drugged and sleeping, which was preferable to being awake. His back and shoulders were sore from lying in bed, and the constant pain from his wounds became an agonised flare if he tried to move, so that he was dependent on the nurses for everything, like an infant. The first time his dressing had been changed, he had unwisely looked down at the lower part of his body and had seen the mangled, clotted mess that stretched from his stomach to his pelvis. Next time, he didn't look. He didn't want to see the damage to the firmly-muscled body he had always taken for granted. He wondered whether he would ever be strong and healthy again, or whether he would have to lie on his back forever, being fed the mess of gruel which was all he could eat.

"You'll be out of the war, any rate," Dobson said, stretching clenched fists.

"I can't remember being in it."

"I wouldn't complain. You're the lucky one. More than I'll be. Patched up and sent back, that's what'll happen to me."

"Likely the war will be over by then."

Dobson laughed, without humour. "Not after this last little lot. No, I was in at the beginning, and I'll be in it to the end – if I don't cop a packet first."

"You're a regular, then?"

"Yes, worse luck. Like most blokes out here. Been in since '11. All parades and mess dinners it was then. A spell in India to look forward to, maybe. Might have thought twice if I'd seen this shooting match coming. What about you? Joined up on a heroic impulse? Funny really. You Irish haven't got much to thank the English for, I wouldn't have thought."

Edward's letter. It was because of Edward he had enlisted.

"*It is a great pity to have to put off returning to*

26

Cambridge," Edward had written, "*but there seems to be little choice. Officers are urgently needed, and with my O.T.C. experience at school it seems selfish to put off enlisting merely because I want to continue my studies.*"

Edward's comments summed up Patrick's own position neatly. He was due to begin his degree course at London University within a few weeks, but every day since the beginning of August he had seen the appeal in the newspaper for volunteers. He didn't want to give up the university place he had worked so hard for, but neither did he want to take an easy option when other young men of his age were clamouring to enlist. He had seen older men, too, men of an age to be married with families, waiting at the local recruiting office. It seemed wrong for him to let others go to war, while he – fitted by education, background, training, even by inclination, to be an officer – stayed behind.

He decided to broach the subject with his father that evening as they set out to walk along Bell Common to the edge of the forest. The big horse-chestnut near the house was already turning from green to dusty gold, and the umbrella-heads of cow parsley which had foamed white along the verge in May and June were sun-browned and dry. The long summer was coming to an end.

"I think," Patrick said carefully, plucking a grass stem, "I ought to enlist, instead of going to University. It seems right."

His father's reaction was predictable, a humph of exasperation, and: "It's England's war, not Ireland's. There's no reason why you should feel obliged to join up."

Patrick saw the flaw in this argument: it didn't seem fair to live in a country, have your son educated there and then say that its need was nothing to do with you. Behind the remark, he knew, lay his father's more personal feeling; as a widower, he did not want his only son to put his life at risk.

"I had a letter from Brendan," Patrick said. "He's going to enlist with the Dublin Fusiliers."

"I don't imagine your uncle can be pleased about it," his father said shortly, stooping to let the setter bitch off the lead. She ran on ahead in her easy loping gait, nose down, her chestnut coat bright against the bleached grasses.

"From what Brendan says, the mood in Dublin is that it's a war on behalf of small nations," Patrick said. "If Ireland helps the British army to free Belgium, she'll have proved her right to independence. Brendan says recruiting's going as well in Ireland as it is here. After all, the more volunteers there are, the sooner the war will end. And by the time the Kitchener recruits get out to France, the regulars will have done most of the job."

"It seems to me that your mind's already made up," his father said.

"I suppose it is."

Patrick was surprised to realise that this was true. Superstitiously, he whistled the setter bitch to him as they approached the Epping Upland road and she bounded towards him, her nose powdered with grass pollen. No, he thought, it wasn't Ireland's war; he would bring loneliness and anxiety to his father if he joined the army: anyone in his position could find a dozen reasons to stay at home. But he knew that any justifications he offered would seem like lame excuses, to himself as well as to others. The letter from Edward seemed to be providing the final push; he would trust Edward's judgement. He had never lost the sense that Edward would always, unfailingly, do the right thing.

He was trying to train himself to ignore the constant pain. Sometimes it worked, if he were drowsy, or could arrange himself in a position which put no strain on his stomach. Having woken abruptly after turning awkwardly in his sleep, he was now wide awake, aware of every sound in the quiet ward: the soft tread of the nurses, the muffled clatter of instruments, low groaning from a bed opposite, a quick urgent command muttered from someone's dream. Apart from the pale glow of a shaded lamp, the ward was in darkness. He wondered what the time was. But what did it really matter? Usually, time could be relied on to pass at a steadily measured pace; here it had little meaning. How long had he been on the hospital ship – days, weeks? He had no idea. All he knew was that when he was awake, and in pain, time seemed barely to pass at all; the frustration and the discomfort gnawed at his nerves. Eventually, he supposed, the ship would berth somewhere on the south coast of England and he would be taken off it. Confined to his bed, he found it hard to believe that he was on a ship at all; only the occasional swaying sensation, which he could barely distinguish from the swimming in his head, or the nurses' slight adjustments of balance as they walked between the beds with loaded trays, seemed to suggest it.

29

"Here. That's a nasty cough. I've brought you some water."

A pale oval face came into focus, dark shadowed eyes looking at him anxiously.

He raised himself on one elbow and took the offered glass. "Thank you."

"Are you in pain?"

"I'll be all right."

The nurse was young and well-spoken, the sort of girl he had seen dressed in smart summer clothes at school Speech Day, watching her brother collect a prize. He wondered what such a girl was doing tending injured men in the Mediterranean. "The war has changed everything," a voice remarked inside his head. Who had said that? He sipped the water, mentally chasing a train of thought he had been trying to follow earlier. When had he last seen Edward? His mind obediently flashed up a picture of Edward in officer's uniform, his face serious, blue eyes shadowed by the peaked cap with the oak-leaf emblem of the Epping Foresters. That had been their last meeting, the mess dinner, when Edward had given him the War Sonnets by Rupert Brooke which had so impressed both of them. But no, he had got it out of order; it had been later than that, after they had been gazetted to separate battalions, when Edward had sent the sonnets in a letter. *Blow out, you bugles, over the rich Dead …*

. . . These laid the world away; poured out the red sweet wine of youth . . . The phrase had stuck in Patrick's mind from his first reading of the poems. Waiting for the troop train to fill up, he unfolded Edward's letter and re-read it.

"I read these in 'New Numbers' and wondered whether you had seen them," Edward had written. *"They seem to catch the present mood so perfectly. I hear that Rupert Brooke is on his way to the Dardanelles – maybe you will see something of him out there . . ."*

Patrick wasn't a connoisseur of poetry like Edward, but he had read the sonnets attentively and now looked at them again. The poems must have been written in the last few months, and in some it was as if Rupert Brooke were speaking to him directly, voicing his own inarticulate thoughts: *Now God be thanked, who has matched us with His hour, And caught our youth, and wakened us from sleeping . . .* Yes, it was timely, to be sure. Patrick knew that Edward regretted not being sent out to the Dardanelles himself; Homer's purple seas and the Mediterranean islands peopled with legendary ghosts would have suited Edward's romantic temperament better than the trenches and barbed wire of the Western Front. It was odd how things had turned out. He would be the first of the two to leave England, destined for the glamour and adventure of the Mediterranean campaign, while Edward, in spite of his eagerness to see active service, was still at officers' training camp in Essex on a signalling course. It had been a blow to both of them that they had been separated after their initial training when Patrick, together with another new second lieutenant, had been chosen to replace a sick officer in a regular battalion. He had asked his commanding officer whether Edward could apply for a transfer, but the Lieutenant Colonel had dismissed the idea.

"I'm afraid I couldn't possibly recommend it. I'm not in favour of friends being posted to the same company. Perhaps you'll understand why when you've seen action."

Patrick was bitterly disappointed. In all his thoughts of enlisting he had imagined himself and Edward crossing the Channel in a troop ship, sharing billets, parading their platoons, going into action together . . . He put Edward's letter away in his pack, and took out his sketch-pad. During the long wait at Charing Cross he had drawn some quick impressions of the crowded platforms, and he took these out now and looked at them.

The other new Lieutenant, Allington, leaned across to see. "Not bad, Paddy. The only thing is, they've invented this wonderful new gadget called the camera. Saves a lot of time and effort."

"Is that so. It's a pity you didn't think to tell me that before."

How much better it would have been, he thought, looking through the window at the muddy, slow-moving Thames as the train pulled out, if Edward had been with him now instead of the rather tedious Allington. All the same, he felt a thrill of excitement at the thought of the journey ahead, and all that lay unforeseeably beyond.

It seemed absurd now that he had barely considered the idea of being killed or injured. And where was Edward, he wondered, turning his head uncomfortably on his pillow; why had it taken so long to occur to him that Edward could be wounded or even dead by this time? News would be slow to travel . . .

Dobson sat down heavily on the edge of his bed and swung his legs up with an grunt of effort. "Did you know this ship was built as sister to the Titanic?"

he remarked to Patrick. "Bloke up on deck just told me."

"That's not very reassuring."

"That's what I said to him. Still, we'll probably be all right. I don't suppose there are too many icebergs floating about the Mediterranean in summer."

Summer. It was already summer. Where had the time gone, what had happened to fill in the blanks in his mind? Still trying to sort out the hopelessly assorted threads of memory that knotted and tangled in his head, he tried to remember the last time he had actually talked to Edward, but found himself thinking instead of a time long before that.

There were rabbits on the Common crouched in the long grass, scuts bobbing as they bounded off at the tread of human feet. Patrick shouted encouragement to the elderly black Labrador as he set off in clumsy pursuit. Silly old Seamus. He hadn't a hope of catching one, and wouldn't know what to do with it if he did. He always came back looking apologetic and waggling his stumpy tail so foolishly that he made Patrick laugh.

It was a still May evening, with only a faint touch of coolness in the air after a warm day. Patrick, on a weekend exeat from school, was aware for the first time of a sense of familiarity with this stretch of common, its grazing cattle and timbered cottages, and the expanse of Epping Forest ahead. Only a few weeks ago, he had considered Essex to be dull and featureless in comparison with the Dublin Mountains he was used to, the countless rounded peaks fading into blue distance, and the sense of airy space above the city and the steel-grey Irish Sea.

But the forest had its attractions: secluded thickets of holly and tall stands of beech and hornbeam, shy fallow deer, narrow tree-arched roads where Dick Turpin had robbed travellers. In the summer vacation, Patrick thought, he'd ask his father to hire horses, and they could ride the whole length and breadth of the forest, to Chingford Plain where Queen Elizabeth had ridden out from her royal hunting lodge. It was several months since he'd last gone riding, and he'd be forgetting how . . .

Realising that he had lost sight of Seamus, he stopped to scan the expanse of grass and brambles, whistling. A motor-car was progressing slowly along the Epping road, raising the dust; it was a sight unfamiliar enough to make Patrick turn and look. The car, an Austin, was driven by a man in tweeds with his face wrapped in a checked scarf in spite of the warmth of the evening. Two cyclists, coming from the London direction, were drawing level by the Epping Upland turn; the car passed them, and Patrick heard the grinding of brakes as it stopped abruptly. One of the cyclists shouted something, and then flung his bicycle down in the dust and ran to the car. An accident? Forgetting the dog, Patrick ran up the slight rise towards the road. The cyclist was stooped over a black shape by the near front wheel of the car.

The shock of recognition jarred Patrick to a standstill.

"Seamus . . ."

No-one heard him. The driver unwound his muffler and told the cyclist in aggrieved tones, "I didn't even see him until he was right under the car. You ought to keep him under control. He could have caused an accident."

The cyclist, a dark-haired boy, said nothing. He stroked the dog's head and ears with gentle fingers. Patrick, drawing closer, saw a trickle of blood from the dog's mouth, already congealing in the warm dust, and the eye glazing in death. He knelt down, and the other boy looked at him.

"Is he your dog?"

"My father's."

"He must have been killed instantly," the boy said. "He could hardly have known anything."

"He probably didn't see the car coming. He was short-sighted." Patrick's eyes blurred as he looked down at Seamus lying so pathetically in the dusty road. A few moments ago he had been blundering about in the long grasses, intent on his pursuit of interesting smells. His muzzle was grey with age and his top lip lifted over his teeth so that he looked as if he were snarling. Patrick didn't want to look any closer, to see where the bleeding came from. He groped in his jacket pocket for a handkerchief.

The motorist had climbed out of the car to look. "An old dog, by the look of him. Better get him out of the road, hadn't you?"

"Come on, Edward," said the other cyclist, a young woman. "We'd better leave our bicycles by the side of the road and help. Where do you live?" she asked Patrick.

"In the first house past the common," Patrick said. "I shall have to tell my father . . ." His voice quavered as he spoke and he felt again in his pockets for the handkerchief which wasn't there.

"Oh, how awful for you," the young woman said

sympathetically. She handed him a handkerchief from her own pocket. The likeness between her and the boy suggested that they were brother and sister; both had thin faces and crisp wavy hair, nearly black, the girl's pinned up untidily beneath a boater. Patrick realised now that he had seen the boy before. He was in his class at school, a rather quiet, clever boy. His name was Sidgwick and he was top of the batting averages, Patrick remembered; he didn't think they had so much as spoken to each other. Collard or Peters would have ragged him mercilessly for crying over a dog, but Sidgwick didn't seem to notice. He straightened up and looked at the car-driver and said, "We'll move him out of your way."

"Yes. Well. Lucky there was no accident caused," the driver said again, settling back into his seat and slamming the door. "I'm sorry about the dog," he added, putting the car into gear.

"We'll come home with you, won't we, Edward?" the girl said to her brother, who gathered the lifeless dog into his arms. The car pulled away slowly, and Patrick followed Sidgwick down to the path across the common and the disturbingly short distance back to the house. Patrick thought of his father where he had left him writing letters in his study, happily unaware, for the last few moments, of what had just happened. How would he tell him?

He blew his nose with Miss Sidgwick's handkerchief and said indistinctly, "It was my fault. I shouldn't have whistled him. I shouldn't have let him get out of my sight."

The girl said nothing, but put her hand on his sleeve as they drew level with the front garden gate. Edward Sidgwick, the dog heavy in his arms, looked round to check that this was the right house, and Patrick pushed the gate open, reluctantly. The lilac bush by the porch scented the air with heavy sweetness. Patrick looked down at the dog's lolling head as Edward followed him through the gate. He saw that a trickle of blood stained the whiteness of Edward's rolled shirtsleeve and smeared the tanned skin of his forearm.

Brendan

The M.O. nodded to the Sister. "Right. You can replace the dressing now. You'd better carry on with the irrigations for a few days longer." Noticing Patrick's expression, he added, "It's unpleasant, I know. But there's still a risk of infection. If we can keep that at bay, you should stand every chance of making a reasonable recovery."

"Will I really? How reasonable?"

"In time, I mean. Wounds like this are slow to heal. You'll be in hospital for a good while when we get back to England. But there's no permanent damage to any vital organs. You've been very lucky."

Luck, Patrick reflected as the M.O. moved on to the next patient, was a matter of degree. How many times had he been told how lucky he was? Lucky to be lying here in bed for days on end with his insides mangled. Lucky to endure the agony of the irrigation treatment at four-hourly intervals. Lucky to be facing a long period of recovery in hospital. But he had seen enough now to recognise that he was indeed lucky. He had watched a young man in the bed opposite die slowly from gas gangrene, with such drawn-out pain that Patrick had been glad when the screens round the bed announced the end. Once gangrene set in, he knew, there was nothing to be done, unless an offending limb could be amputated. What would it be like to face the rest of your life with an arm or a leg missing, or even both legs, or with a horribly disfigured face? A glance around the ward put his own suffering into perspective.

"Give me the scissors, please, Nurse," the Sister said, deftly unwrapping a roll of lint. Her manner always made Patrick suspect that she saw him as a parcel to be wrapped and tied up and disposed of. The younger nurse stood by with the tray of instruments, an expression of sympathetic concern on her face. Patrick noticed for the first time that she was rather pretty, and felt a stab of embarrassment at being compelled to lie beneath her gaze like a skinned carcase on a butcher's chopping board. He told himself that she must be used to such sights, and far worse. She would soon be as hardened to it as the middle-aged Sister.

"When will we get back to England?" he asked.

"Two or three days," the Sister said. "Sooner than you should. Finish this dressing for me, nurse, while I get started on the next." She laid the lint pad firmly in place, ignoring Patrick's sharp intake of breath, and followed the M.O. to the next bed.

"What did she mean by that?" he asked, puzzled.

The young nurse was cutting lengths of bandage, laying them out ready. "I think she meant that by rights, you should have been left in the Malta hospital, until you'd got past this stage. But it was so crowded there with all the operations and the dysentery cases." She began bandaging over the lint pad. "I'm sorry if this hurts."

"Not nearly as much as when Sister does it . . ."

The nurse looked quickly over her shoulder to check that the Sister hadn't heard, and then smiled. "At least you should get home to Ireland more quickly than if you'd stayed in Malta. Perhaps you'll be sent to a convalescent hospital there."

One journey home had always stayed in his mind with particular clarity. It was the long-awaited first day of the summer vacation, and he and Edward were on board the steamer, standing on deck looking across at the hazy distance which separated Wales from Ireland. Patrick squinted into the fading sunlight, unsure whether a dim smudge on the horizon was the Irish coast or a trick of his eyesight. In his mind, he could clearly picture Kingstown Harbour, and Dublin's River Liffey and the Rathmines suburb where his cousins lived. He had made the journey several times before, but to Edward everything so far had been new, from the splendour of the Snowdonia mountains, glimpsed from the train, to the comings and goings of passengers, freight and livestock at Holyhead.

If it hadn't been for Patrick's alternative plan, Edward would have spent the school vacation with an elderly aunt in Colchester while his parents visited various sanatoria on the Continent for Dr Sidgwick's medical research. Patrick could still hardly believe it, that the suggestion he had made so tentatively was soon to become reality: Edward was going to spend the whole summer holiday with him and his cousins. His pleasure at the prospect was marred only by a fear that Edward and Brendan wouldn't take to each other. Mary, the eldest cousin, would like Edward, he was certain, and Cathal was too young to matter much; of Brendan he was less sure. Brendan would make up his own mind. He wouldn't take a liking to someone just to be amenable.

The wind became cold as the ship pulled out from the shelter of the harbour, sending chill fingers down their necks and making their eyes water. Patrick's father retreated to the comfort of the salon, while the two boys buttoned up their jackets and stayed on deck to watch for gannets and shearwaters. At last the green-blue smudge of the coast defined itself into cliffs and hills and recognisable settlements, and the ship approached Kingstown, with its ring of hills and the lights strung out around the harbour in the dusk, and the Bailey light flashing a welcome across the calm glimmering water.

"A warning, really, not a welcome. But it seems like one," Patrick said, as they waited to disembark. The summer evening was warm, the air carrying salt and a fishy tang and a spicy odour of gorse from the hills. Patrick's father, rejoining the two boys, inhaled deeply, his ritual first intake of Irish air, like an alcoholic entering a tap-room.

Ireland. Home.

"No," he said to the nurse. "My home isn't in Ireland. Not any more."

She assembled her instruments in the tray and rearranged his blankets and pillow. "It sounds as if you're sad about that. Would you like to go back there?"

"I would." The conviction in his voice surprised

41

him. For all his British patriotism at the outbreak of war, he was Irish still and would always think of himself as Irish. Yes, he would return.

"Perhaps you will, one day. That's all finished then. Try to get some sleep now."

He had desperately wanted Brendan and Edward to be friends.

He should have known that it was too much to expect. There was no difficulty with the rest of the family: Aunt Margaret, relaxed and informal; Uncle James, smelling as usual of oil and turpentine, his mind occupied with the portrait he was working on; Mary, a young woman now, looking more like her mother than Patrick remembered; eleven-year-old Cathal, thin and gangly as a colt, excited at having the house full of visitors. Brendan kept his distance. Since they had last met, Patrick, though a year younger, had overtaken him in height, while Edward was two or three inches taller still; Brendan had filled out, with the stocky build likely to become thick-set in adulthood. He was altered in other ways too. His boyish confidence had changed to an air of guarded resolution; his brown eyes, light amber in colour, not dark like Patrick's own, seemed to take in everything, though he said little. He greeted Edward warily on the first night and hardly spoke to him for the next two days.

Patrick, his doubts justified, realised that he should have known. Brendan would instinctively dislike Edward because he was English, and because he represented all that Brendan despised in the English. And Edward was reserved, difficult to get to know. After four or five years, Patrick thought that he probably knew him as well as anyone did; Edward preferred the intimacy of a close friendship to the easy sociability of a group. He did not give away his loyalty or his affection indiscriminately. Patrick liked him all the more for that, but he saw too that Edward's polite, distant manner could be taken for aloofness. To Brendan, it would appear as superiority.

Late on the third evening, Brendan sat reading the newspaper in a corner of the sitting-room while Patrick and Edward played chess. Patrick, about to be out-manoeuvred, wondered whether to suggest that Edward played Brendan. He was not sure how good an idea it was. Edward would almost certainly win, increasing Brendan's resentment. Gazing rather desperately at the board, he wondered whether it were too late to bring his remaining bishop to the rescue of his king. He looked up, and saw that Brendan was watching the game carefully, in spite of pretending to be absorbed in his newspaper article.

Patrick brought the bishop over to cover his queen, wondering whether Brendan had seen a better move. But instead of commenting, his cousin said suddenly, to Edward, "What do you think of the Home Rule Bill? Will it go through, do you think?"

Edward's long fingers rested briefly on the king's crown as he considered his next move. He changed his mind, and moved his knight instead before answering. Patrick knew that he recognised Brendan's question as a challenge.

"It must go through, this time," Edward said. "I hope it does. The Irish have every right to Home

Rule. Ulster will have to comply, and forget its differences."

Brendan, who had clearly been expecting a different answer, was silenced for the moment. Patrick turned his attention back to the board, and the innocuous-seeming knight. He couldn't see what Edward was up to. He sat forward, elbows on his knees, frowning at the chessmen.

There was a silence filled only by the soft hiss of the gas lamp until Brendan spoke again. "The only thing is," he remarked, "Home Rule isn't enough. Just a sop to keep us quiet. We want complete independence. An Irish Republic."

"That's not true, Brendan." Mary, who was mending a blouse, had been sitting so quietly in the corner opposite her brother that she might not have been present. "Not to say *we*. That's not the way most people think."

"Ah, I know. I've been listening to too many inflammatory speeches. You sound like Mother." Brendan slumped back in his chair in exasperation.

Mary, looking as hurt as a pupil reprimanded unfairly in class, continued darning. Edward turned to her. "What do you think?"

"I think . . ." She seemed surprised to be addressed by him so directly. "I think most people will be well satisfied with Home Rule. It's what we've been waiting for, these few years . . ."

Edward's eyes were fixed attentively on her face as she spoke. Patrick saw, to his surprise, a slow blush creep from her neck over her face. She was aware of it, too; she stopped speaking abruptly and bent over the soft pale fabric of the blouse she was mending. Was it her sense of defying her brother, or . . . Patrick was confused by the undercurrents of tension in the room. He looked across at Edward, who seemed to realise that he had unintentionally embarrassed Mary and was studying the chess-board again, leaning on the table with his chin cupped in his hand. The light from the standard-lamp behind gave him a look of nobility, like a figure hewn out of stone, a young god contemplating the infinite. His eyes were as blue as a Siamese cat's, a striking contrast with his dark, nearly black, hair. Was Mary's shyness with him because she . . . ? Patrick could hardly frame the thought. Mary was eighteen, more or less an adult, and Edward almost two years younger, still a schoolboy . . .

Brendan said sharply, "It always takes a minority, to lead the way. The rest will follow. People sometimes need to be told what it is they want."

"You may be right there. Think of the women's suffrage movement," Edward said. "The suffragists are mocked and jeered at, but when the government finally comes to its senses everyone will thank them for what they've done."

Brendan raised his eyebrows. "You think the government will give in?"

"Yes, eventually. It's obviously ridiculous not to grant women the vote."

"When did being ridiculous ever worry the British government?"

Edward looked up quickly, then deflected the barbed comment by grinning and saying lightly, "I expect you're right. I suppose there would be votes for women in an Irish Republic?"

"Would? You mean will. But we've a whole nation to free from slavery first."

"I think," Edward said carefully, "the two causes go hand in hand." He moved his rook to threaten Patrick's bishop.

Mary stood up abruptly, putting her bundle of sewing on a low table. "I think I'll make some more tea and then turn in. It's getting late."

Brendan, Edward and himself, Patrick thought, lying awake and staring into the darkness. Remembering that summer vacation four years ago was like thinking about three complete strangers. So much had happened since; much of it he could only guess at, his memory still refusing to fill in the more recent blanks. Edward could be anywhere – safely at home in Essex, or in some godforsaken trench on the Western Front, or in hospital, or . . . Brendan was still, as far as Patrick knew, back in Ireland, but for how long? What were the chances, he thought gloomily, of all three of them surviving the war?

It was so stuffy in the ward that his lungs felt clogged; the sheet underneath him was sticky and crumpled. He wriggled and fidgeted into a slightly more comfortable position. Someone else was restless, too; he heard movement close by.

"Leary? Are you awake too?" Will Dobson said in a stage whisper.

"Yes, I am."

"Bloody hot, isn't it?"

"All these sweaty bodies . . ."

"Still, we'll be out of it by this time tomorrow. Back in dear old Blighty."

"Tomorrow?"

"That's right. Funny, isn't it, how time flies when you're enjoying yourself. Cheer up, old chap. A change of scene will do you good. Strikes me we could do quite well out of it."

"How do you mean?"

Dobson struck a match, and the flare of flame illuminated his cupped hand and the lower half of his face, making him look for an instant like some penitent in a religious painting. He lit a cigarette and breathed in deeply. "Wounded hero and all that. A bit of sympathy and admiration would go down a treat."

Waiting for Edward

Carried off the ship by stretcher, Patrick looked
back at it from the Southampton quayside. It
dwarfed the harbour, long and low, with three
funnels, and red crosses above the water-line to
show that it was a hospital ship. Like its ill-fated
sister, he remembered, it had been built as a luxury
liner; its decks should have been thronged with
passengers in elegant clothes, with parasols, and
monogrammed pigskin luggage. The passengers it
carried now wore hospital pyjamas or bandages
or convalescent suits of grey. Those able to walk
were making their own way along the quayside to
the waiting ambulances, while orderlies carried the
stretcher cases. A number of people had gathered
to greet the arrivals, but the atmosphere was sober,
nothing like the scene which flashed into Patrick's
mind as he realised that he had been here before:
he had walked from the station to the harbour
through cheering crowds who waved flags and
surged forward to press cigarettes or money into the
hands of the departing troops. The few civilians now
present were subdued into quietness, outnumbered,
shocked perhaps by the unending lines which filed

down the gangplanks and congested the quay with a wedge of wounded humanity.

It was the middle of the night when the convoy arrived at its destination, a military hospital in south London. The journey had seemed to take forever: ambulance, train, ambulance again. The hospital train had shunted slowly, unbearably slowly through the night, gathering speed for a short while, then lurching to a stop. To Patrick, accustomed to the gentle swaying motion of the ship, every movement jarred, until he found himself clenching his fists uselessly against the pain. The medical staff on the train were kept busy, hurrying up and down between the narrow bunks to attend to a haemorrhage at one end of the carriage, a delirious patient at the other.

Patrick had looked forward to arriving in London as a significant stage in his recovery. Instead, he was drained, wrung out with pain and exhaustion. He had to be given morphia again, a stage he thought he had passed.

"It's the journey. It was too much for you, I shouldn't wonder," said a cheerful staff nurse, plumping up his pillow. "They shouldn't have sent you back so soon. You'll feel a lot better after a good long rest."

He felt as if he had been lying in bed for months, watching the days and nights pass. His legs and feet must be withering with disuse, he thought, wriggling his toes to check that they were still alive. His body seemed to have become a useless attachment, made up of aches and pains and too-slowly healing flesh.

Gradually recovering from his stupor enough to

take notice of his surroundings, he saw that he was in a long narrow ward, with windows, unfamiliar to him after the ship. Through the glass he could see the tops of plane trees, already fading from their summer colours.

"What month is it?" he asked an orderly.

The elderly man laughed. "September, mate. Where've you been?"

It was a surgical ward, filled with patients recovering from various injuries and operations. Only a few had been out at the Dardanelles; the rest talked about the Western Front, their conversation scattered with place-names strange to Patrick: Festubert, Cambrin, Givenchy. The war was still going on, of course; he realised that he had little idea of what was happening. He noticed that the man in the next bed was reading a newspaper. When he put it down, Patrick asked, "Could I have a look at that?"

"'Course. Here you are. It's a few days old, mind. Somebody's probably got today's."

The headlines told of a new campaign at Loos, near the Belgian border, and of a renewed assault on the Gallipoli peninsula, by British troops and ANZACs. The name conjured up a picture of men in slouch hats, grinning, sun-tanned; frowned upon by the British command for their slackness about saluting and other minor points of discipline . . . "Never mind what the Colonial troops get up to. You're officers in the British Army. We have different standards. Fraternisation must be kept to a minimum." A clipped accent, tetchy, very English . . . the voice from his memory was so clear that it seemed to be barking in his ear. Where,

50

when? Patrick frowned at the newspaper, reading of new landings at Suvla Bay, an ANZAC assault on Chunuk Bair. Those names . . .

Someone had set up a gramophone at the far end of the ward; the music it played, a syncopated piano rag, nagged at the edges of his consciousness. The fragment of memory slipped away as he tried to grasp it. It was like a blind coming down, blank. Too tired to read any more, he handed the newspaper back to its owner.

Much later he awoke from a deep sleep, his ears slowly attuning to the low hum of conversation. There were visitors in the ward, people in civilian clothes; more arrivals came through the double doors with armfuls of flowers, anxious eyes scanning the rows of faces, while others were already seated around beds. Still drowsy, Patrick listened to snatches of conversation. For the first time it occurred to him that he might be able to expect visitors himself . . . his father . . . did he know what had happened, where he was? He wished he had thought of sending a card. How did you get hold of postcards or writing paper, and stamps?

In the bed opposite Patrick's was a young man with his head bandaged, who sat up gazing desperately at the entrance to the ward. With each new unrecognised visitor his face took on a look of deeper and deeper disappointment, until he seemed on the point of crumpling into tears. Patrick wondered who he was expecting; his wife? No, he looked too young to be married. A girl-friend, then? Patrick began to watch the doors with almost equal anxiety, checking across the ward for a response each time a likely-looking person entered, hoping that the other man's feverish anticipation would not be in vain. At last a Red Cross volunteer approached from the other side of the bed, making the young man jump.

"Here you are, mate. Letter for you."

The young man took the letter and stared at it for a moment, then tore open the envelope and began to read the pages inside, holding them close to his face and turning over the sheets rapidly as if he could not take in their contents fast enough. Patrick, fascinated, was diverted when the Red Cross man came over to him and handed him a letter.

"Lieutenant Leary? One for you too."

Surprised, Patrick took the envelope expecting to see his father's handwriting. Instead, he saw that it was addressed in Edward's spiky black script. Inside was a short note:

"Dear Patrick, I came to see you today but wasn't allowed in as you were too ill. Will come back tomorrow (Tuesday) and hope to see you then. Regards, Edward."

Patrick read the note through three times and then slumped back against his pillow, almost dizzy with relief. It was all right, then: Edward was safe and alive, and not only that but here in London . . . they would be meeting soon, talking, exchanging news . . . Until now it had been more than he dared hope for, but already it began to seem like something expected. Edward had always been good at putting things right, for as long as they had known each other.

He had looked out for Edward Sidgwick on his return to school after the exeat. Edward slept in

52

another dormitory, and so Patrick didn't see him again until breakfast on Monday morning and the Latin lesson which followed. He was disappointed when Edward showed no sign of recognition, as if nothing had happened. For Patrick, the memory of Seamus' death was as painful as an open sore; he thought Edward might have shown some interest in what had happened after he and his sister had left. Quite unable to concentrate on irregular verbs, Patrick drew a little picture in the margin of his book: the freshly-dug grave at the bottom of the garden beneath the flowering cherry, the mound of earth on which he had spelled out SEAMUS in white stones and planted a sprig of heather.

Edward was apparently fully absorbed in the lesson, answering the teacher's questions confidently, and always, Patrick noticed, accurately. He seemed to be a quiet, independent boy, with no particular friend in the class. Patrick was not sure what he thought of him. Perhaps Edward was aloof and unfriendly, secure in his awareness of his academic strengths.

It was not until later in the week that they spoke to each other again. Patrick, setting out his books and papers for evening prep, was surprised when Edward walked along the row and sat down at the adjoining desk. At the end of the ninety minutes, when they were collecting their things together, Edward spoke to him rather diffidently.

"Some people in the village at home have got a litter of puppies. Red setters. I thought you might like one . . . for your father. If you'd like it, I could get you one. They'll be needing homes."

"Red setters?"

"Yes. From a family of working dogs. They're not pedigree. But if your father likes Labradors he'd probably like setters as well. It's just an idea." Edward trailed off rather defensively, as if he thought he had been too forward.

"A puppy! It's a grand idea," Patrick said. "I could surprise him with it. A surprise present. Can I really have one? Would they be ready to leave their mother?"

Edward seemed pleased that his idea met with such enthusiasm. "Not until the summer vac," he said, and then, after a moment, "You could come and look at them meanwhile though, next time you're at home. If you'd like to. You could choose the one you want. We don't live far from you, in Littlehays. Have you got a bicycle?"

"My father has. I could borrow that."

"That's easy then. Next time you go home."

The room was nearly empty. Edward smiled briefly and then turned to hurry after the last stragglers, as if he had already spent too long in conversation. Patrick, surprised, recovered in time to call, "Thank you. I'd like that," after the retreating figure.

It was Edward's way, he soon learned, to make a gesture of friendship and then withdraw. A few days later, when lessons had finished for the afternoon, Edward came over to Patrick's desk and said, "Some of us are going out to the cricket nets. Would you like to come?"

"I'm not very good at cricket."

Edward grinned. "Well, that's what net practice is for, isn't it?"

"No, I meant . . ." Patrick felt foolish. "I don't know much about it. All the rules."

Edward suddenly bent forward, looking closely at the open notebook on Patrick's desk. "Did you draw that in the lesson just now?"

"I did." Patrick pulled the book towards him and closed the pages. He wasn't sure that Edward would approve of wasting time in the lesson by sketching the master. The maths master, an earnest young man with a thin bony nose and straggly hair which he tried in vain to keep tidy, was an easy target. Patrick had learned that he could win popularity with some of the other boys through his deftness at caricature, but he didn't think Edward would be so easily impressed. In any case, it wasn't one of his best drawings.

Edward just said, "It's a very good likeness, but I shouldn't let Mr Balderson catch you at it. You needn't worry about not being good at cricket. There's only me and Bates and Hingcliffe. We'll coach you, if you like."

"Well, I will then. Thanks for asking."

Edward seemed to be good at everything, Patrick thought with some envy as he stood awkwardly at the crease. Edward's movements were graceful and athletic as he ran in to bowl, aiming the ball expertly. Patrick, misjudging the first ball, took a wild swipe, and the bails clattered to the ground.

"I'm no good at all." He was annoyed with himself, sure that the other boys must be laughing at him. "I'm more use with a hurley."

"You'll be all right," Edward said. He picked the ball up from the side netting and came up to the crease. "It's your stance that's all wrong.

Look, stand like this, with your feet facing that way. Here . . . turn your shoulders, that's better, that'll give you a better swing. Your leading wrist needs to be a bit further forward . . . yes. Now don't rush at the ball this time, keep your eye on it, and take a steadier stroke . . ."

Concentrating hard, and following Edward's patient instructions, Patrick soon found that he could hit the ball a satisfying crack, and could even begin to exert some control over its direction. By the end of the session, he had had a go at bowling and had caught out Hingcliffe with a pleasingly spectacular leap. Cricket, he decided, might not be so bad after all.

"At this rate," Edward said as they walked back across the long-shadowed playing-field, "we'll have you in the junior eleven by the end of the season."

"You don't mean that?"

"Yes, I do. I can see you turning into a really useful player."

When the Red Cross worker made his way round the ward again, handing out cups of tea this time, Patrick asked for a pen.

"What's this hospital called?" he asked, remembering that he would need to give details.

"1st London General, mate. Camberwell."

Patrick wrote a quick note to his father and addressed it. He wondered how Edward had known where to find him; possibly his father already knew where he was, too, and was already on his way . . .

"Want me to put that in the post for you?" the obliging Red Cross man asked.

"Thank you. Do you know how I could get some

56

more writing-paper? But I haven't got any money," he added as an afterthought.

"I expect you've got a few coins in with your other belongings. Have you got one of them bags? Here it is, look." The man bent to the floor and straightened up holding a standard-issue fabric bag, which he handed over.

"I'd forgotten about that. The nurse took out my razor and other stuff and put it where I can reach it. I suppose there might be some money in there." Patrick opened the bag and examined the contents. There was his pay-book, a few pound notes and some coins, his fountain pen, two pencils, a letter and some folded sheets of paper. He gave the man half a crown for the writing-pad and handed back the borrowed pen.

"Thank you very much."

"No trouble. We've got writing-paper, one of the volunteers comes round with things for sale every morning, only you was asleep today. I'll get it for you as soon as I've finished with the tea."

He went off with his trolley, and Patrick took the letter out of the bag, surprised to see his own handwriting on the envelope. It was addressed to Lt. E. Sidgwick, 5th Epping Foresters. He turned it over, baffled, his first thought to hand it straight to Edward when he came in to visit. Then he realised that he had no idea at all what was in it. The envelope was not sealed; he took out three sheets of paper covered in his own loopy scrawl.

"Dear Edward," he read, *"By the time you read this I shall have gone into action. I am not allowed to tell you the details, although everyone here seems to know all about it, including local shopkeepers*

and fishermen! We are camped outside Alexandria, having briefings, briefings and more briefings. There are troops here from all sorts of places – Australians, New Zealanders, French, Sikhs and Gurkhas. The ANZACs seem determined to enjoy themselves while they wait, and our staff are trying to keep us away from them in case we pick up their casual attitudes! They are very friendly to us whenever we meet them, and seem to be even more patriotically British than the British, if that's possible. They are on far easier terms with their superior officers than we are, and even call them by their Christian names. Our brass hats would have apoplexy!

Everyone seems very confident that the campaign will be successful, and if weight of number is anything to go by, it will be. There are bound to be casualties, but it seems best not to think too much about that.

It is very warm here even though it is only April, and I should think it will be unbearably hot later in the summer. I wish you could have been out here too. It is so exciting, both the prospect of going into action, and just being here, on the edge of a new continent. Being in Alexandria is like going back far into the past. I have done a few sketches which I shall keep and show you whenever we meet next. It would be marvellous to go further down the Nile, to Cairo and the pyramids, but I'm sure there won't be an opportunity. You would have loved the voyage out, too. A lot of the men were seasick in the Bay of Biscay, but once we got past Gibraltar the voyage was calm and full of interest. We passed the Rock of Gibraltar at night, a huge hulking cliff with lights all over it, and then on into the dawn – rosy-fingered dawn, as Homer described it! It sounds silly, but I keep thinking *of Jason and the Argonauts and Aeneas, and Anthony and Cleopatra, and all the places Odysseus went to before he got home to Ithaca. There is something about the colours here, the clear blue sea and the islands like golden sea creatures, that makes you think of all the old legends. That reminds me – Rupert Brooke is out here! Someone recognised him in Cairo. I wonder if he will publish a new set of sonnets after this campaign? It is curious to think that I will almost be sharing the experiences he writes about.*

I must finish for now, as it is time to get ready for parade. I will write a bit more though before I post this, when there is more to report."

Reaching the abrupt end of the letter, Patrick lay back against the pillows and stared at the ceiling. He felt jarred by the strangeness of reading a letter from himself; the lines of confident looped writing seemed to have been written by a stranger. He closed his eyes, and the scenes he had described in the letter began to develop in his mind like pictures on photographic plate. Narrow crowded streets of sand-coloured limestone, the spreading Nile delta, lines of tents stretching out into the desert. Alexandria. The Colonel he had almost remembered earlier, briefing the junior officers. Rows and rows of troops, embarking for their voyage to the Gallipoli peninsula; the Eastern Mediterranean crowded with naval ships, fishing boats, troop carriers, cargo boats, every kind of vessel imaginable. Mudros harbour, the sun setting in a blaze of gold over the peaks to the west. To the east, an austere, cone-shaped mountain on the Gallipoli peninsula itself, identified by one of the senior officers as Achi Baba. For some reason, the name sent a shiver down Patrick's spine as he stood by the gunwale looking up at its stern heights. Troops, and more troops, by the thousand, amassing for the landings, till it seemed that half the entire Allied army must be there at Mudros. And then, shutting off the crowding memories, the blind closed down, blank.

Red Sweet Wine

Patrick's attention was caught first by the familiarity of Edward's tall figure as he entered the ward, then by something else, something indefinably different. He saw Edward's eyes scanning the ward, and raised a hand to attract his attention. Edward seemed to recognise him with something of a shock. He walked up to the bed and embraced Patrick briefly.

"Pat, I thought I'd never find you in this vast place."

"How did you know where to come?"

"I saw your name in the casualty lists and I found out where you were from Regimental Headquarters . . ."

"There's a chair there . . ."

They were both being very formal, very British, Patrick thought, making polite conversation, while each took in a first impression of the other. Edward was unable to conceal his dismay, making Patrick wonder exactly how his appearance struck someone who had last seen him fit and healthy. And Edward looked different, too, thinner and tired, and his blue eyes looked strained. He brought the chair over and sat down.

"Where have you come from?" Patrick asked.

"I'm on leave. I've been to visit Lorna and then I'm going on home from here. I got back from France the day before yesterday."

"You've been at the front itself, then – in action?"

"Yes. But what about you? They said yesterday that you were worn out by the journey."

"I'm all right."

"You're obviously not all right. Look at you. You look terrible."

Patrick laughed, and then stopped abruptly as the stitches across his stomach pulled. "Thank you. That's exactly what I need to cheer me up. A real boost to morale."

Edward grinned too, wryly. "Sorry. I meant . . . you've obviously been through it . . . How bad is it? I mean . . . anything lasting?"

"They say not. It will take a long time, that's all."

"Pat, I didn't realise it was as bad as this," Edward said quietly. "A minor wound was what I expected, from what they told me yesterday . . . just a small setback after the travelling . . ."

"I suppose," Patrick said, "compared to what other people have got to put up with, this is a minor wound."

"Are you in pain?"

"Not so much, now."

Edward said nothing for a moment, but sat fiddling with the hem of his uniform jacket, his face troubled. Then he said, "So you'll be out of the war for good? Perhaps it's better to be wounded now than to be . . ." He broke off, and for a second Patrick glimpsed anguish beneath his veneer of composure, before he recovered himself with a visible effort. "What was it like, out there? I don't believe what the newspapers say."

"I honestly can't remember." He saw Edward's look of disbelief, and said, "I really can't. Not the landing itself. Things are coming back to me, slowly, but I still don't know how I copped this lot."

Edward seemed about to say something, but then looked away abruptly and took a tin of cigarettes out of his pocket.

"Is it all right to smoke in here?"

"Yes, go ahead."

"Have one?"

"No, thanks. The Sister would have a fit, and I don't know how my insides would react."

"You really can't remember what happened?"

"About the assault on Gallipoli, nothing at all. Most of what I can remember is in here." He reached across to the bedside table and handed over the envelope. "Sorry it's been opened. I read it myself yesterday."

While Edward read the letter from Patrick's other, optimistic self, Patrick watched him closely. He wondered what could have happened to Edward in France to have produced this air of tenseness, this self-control which seemed too brittle to be convincing. It was as if they spoke to each other across a vast gulf, as if their different experiences had penetrated like deep faults in the earth's surface, uncrossable.

When Edward had finished reading, he flung the sheets of paper down on the bedclothes.

"Red sweet wine of youth," he quoted expressionlessly. *"Now, God be thanked who has matched us with His hour* . . . You know Rupert Brooke's dead, I suppose?"

"*No?*"

"He died out there in the Dardanelles, from blood-poisoning. Before the landings. He's buried on Skyros. Fitting, I suppose. Romantic. Like Shelley or Byron. He didn't live to see what it's really like."

"Well," Patrick said carefully, "What is it really like?"

Edward didn't reply straight away. He sat smoking and staring across the ward. At last he said, "Well, I don't know if it's a good idea to talk about it – if you're shell-shocked. They can cure people's bodies in here, to some extent at any rate, but what about minds? You can't see the wounds, but they're there all the same."

"I haven't thought of it like that. But do tell me. I want to know. You haven't even told me where you were."

Edward stubbed his cigarette butt on the tin-lid and immediately took out another. "At Loos," he said. "A mining area, near the Belgian border, all pit-heads and coal-tips. Not the most picturesque part of France. And it certainly wasn't picturesque afterwards –"

Patrick remembered the newspaper headlines. "Loos? You mean where the attack was?"

"Yes. A decisive manoeuvre that was going to show the Germans just what they were up against. Like the Dardanelles, damn Winston Churchill and his clever ideas. The problem was, they showed us."

"But the newspaper said there had been significant gains," Patrick said.

Edward laughed, humourlessly. "Yes. The newspapers are good at reporting what they think people want to hear. The true story wasn't fit to print. It was a shambles. Our artillery was meant to pulverise the Germans in their trenches before we went over. That didn't happen. We went over and were scythed down by machine-gun fire. They were ready and waiting. God knows how I got out of it without so much as a scratch."

Edward struck a match and held it up to his cigarette, and Patrick saw the flame quiver in his unsteady hand. Edward went on, "One platoon of the Middlesex got through the German wire. Not a single one of them survived. And our company lost five officers, all killed. Five. Just cut down in the open. And then there was the gas."

"The Germans used gas?"

"No. We used it. It drifted back over our trenches and killed dozens of our own men. You can imagine the chaos – companies trying to advance into the machine-gun fire, others trying to run back to escape the gas . . . wounded and dying everywhere . . ."

"Get down, find some cover, here, dig in, dig in . . ."

"We can't last out here, sir, let's get the men back to the boats . . .

" . . . Help that man, someone . . ."

"No time for that – dig in, for Christ's sake, before we're shot to pieces . . ."

Edward's voice seemed to come to him from a long way off. "Are you sure you're all right, Pat? Should I call a nurse or something?"

He opened his eyes and blinked. Edward was gripping his arm and looking at him in concern. He stared back vacantly.

"No, no. I'm all right. Go on. You were telling me about . . . about the gas . . ."

Edward looked doubtful. "Are you sure you really want to hear any more?"

"I do. Please."

"Well . . . A lot of people had been looking *forward* to it –"

Patrick tried to listen, while the fragment of memory nagged at him like a guilty conscience. It was like the shutter of a camera opening, recording a brief, out-of-context glimpse, and no more . . .

" . . . thinking it would be more exciting than the weeks we'd spent in trench routine . . ." Edward talked on, lighting cigarette after cigarette until Patrick, hardly able to breathe the smoke-filled air, wished he would stop. He could not remember Edward smoking before, but the habit seemed obsessive; he drew on each new cigarette as if it were a calming drug. At last he pulled himself up and said, "I'm sorry. You should have stopped me talking on."

"No, I wanted to know. I asked, didn't I?"

"It's awful to see you like this, laid up. But I'm glad you're out of it, Pat."

Edward, Patrick thought, was not out of it. A short stay at home with his family, a few short days, and he would be going back to France, back to the chaos he had described. And under those circumstances, would a stay at home cause more tensions than it dissolved? Edward's parents could hardly fail to notice the change in their son, Patrick thought, looking at his friend's taut expression. Would they understand?

"What will you do while you're at home?" he asked.

"I expect my parents will have things arranged.

They generally do. And . . ." Edward hesitated, flicking ash into a saucer. "There's someone I want to see, very much. A girl, I mean."

"A girl?" Patrick heard the astonishment in his voice, and wondered why he was so taken by surprise. It wasn't out of the question, after all, for Edward to be interested in a girl.

Edward seemed half embarrassed, half amused by Patrick's reaction. "She lives in the village," he continued. "I've known her since we were both children. Recently I've . . . become very fond of her. We've been writing to each other since I've been away. She's a VAD nurse. Before the war she worked for the Morlands, as a maid."

"I see," Patrick said slowly.

Edward gave him a shrewd look. "Yes, I expect you do. Mother doesn't approve, of course."

"No, I suppose not." From his intermittent acquaintance with Mrs Sidgwick, Patrick knew what a formidable species of parent she was. She expected outstanding achievements from her children, and it was lucky for Edward that so far he had been able to fulfil her demands. She had almost despaired of her daughter, Lorna, who had broken away from convention by insisting on a university education and becoming a women's suffrage campaigner; now her hopes and ambitions were now firmly centred on Edward. Before the war, he was to have been a brilliant student at Cambridge. Now that war had intervened, he must be a heroic officer; Mrs Sidgwick would expect Edward to emerge from the trenches with a Military Cross at least. And Patrick had no doubt that an advantageous society marriage in a few years' time would be part of Mrs Sidgwick's plan for her son. For Edward to be romantically involved with a working-class girl would be nothing short of scandalous.

"What worries me more than Mother, though," Edward said, "is whether it's fair on Alice . . . on any girl . . . to encourage any sort of intimacy under these circumstances, when anything could happen. What do you think?"

Patrick, who had never been in a position to consider such a problem, thought about it briefly. He was more taken aback than he cared to admit by this new development in his friend's affairs. He was aware of a quite unjustified feeling of resentment towards this unknown Alice, not because she was working-class but because of her hold on Edward's affections. Aware that this reaction was hardly generous, he tried to push the feeling aside and to consider Edward's question.

"I don't really know," he said at last. "I can see what you mean – you might want to spare her the worry. But then, she has the choice, as well as you – she must know the risks. And for you to like her, she must be someone special. I hope so."

"Yes. She is. I hope you'll meet her one day." Edward grinned suddenly, looking more his old self. "I'm sorry, Pat. I came here to see you and all I've done is talk about myself."

"It's all right. I'm glad you told me all this. I haven't got much to tell you, have I?"

"What will you do, when you're fit to leave here?"

"Go home, I suppose," Patrick said. "Do my degree, perhaps . . . I don't know. Everything seems irrelevant except the war, doesn't it? I feel like a cheat, getting myself out of it."

"You could do some sort of war work. Some kind of office job, administration."

"Perhaps." Patrick didn't want to think about it yet. "Have you heard anything from Brendan at all?" he asked. "I wonder whether he's out in France too, or still back in Ireland? The trouble was, out in the Mediterranean, I heard nothing from anybody."

Edward stared at him, and again Patrick caught the impression of barely-controlled panic.

"But – but – I thought you must have known . . ."

Beached

Dusk fell slowly over Mudros, so that the flaming Asian peaks to the east faded into indigo-shadowed distance and became worldly again. The flat-bottomed boat carried its load of men from the Epping Foresters away from the wooden fishing pier, across the calm waters of the harbour towards the troop-ship. The troops were packed in like penned sheep, shoulder to shoulder, faces expressing excitement, anxiety or boredom, depending on temperament. Patrick, his feet braced against the slight swell, looked out across the breadth of the natural harbour. The scene struck him as faintly unreal, the massed ships looking like a modern Armada in the afterglow of the sunset . . .

Gregory Allington, wedged next to Patrick, jabbed an elbow into his ribs. "Wingfield's turned green already," he said, prosaically, "and we're not even out of the harbour yet."

Patrick looked across at the young captain, who was indeed looking pale and uncomfortable.

"If he's seasick in Mudros Harbour," he said in an undertone, "it's not surprising he had such a bad time of it in the Bay of Biscay."

"He's going to have to stick it out for a few hours yet," Allington said, with evident relish.

Patrick thought of the hours ahead, waiting in the hold of the troop-ship. The fleet would sail at midnight; thinking of what tomorrow would bring made his stomach knot fiercely with fear or excitement, he hardly knew which. The landings had been rehearsed again and again until he knew every detail by heart, but the evening was so tranquil that he found it hard to imagine the Aegean tranquillity shattered by explosive dawn. Fancifully, he pictured the River Clyde as a modern Trojan horse, carrying thousands of men to the Gallipoli peninsula. But the Turks would not welcome the ship, rush to meet it as the Trojans had greeted the wooden horse; by dawn, the Turkish army would have been obliterated, their fortified ridges and cliffs pulverised by shellfire from the Navy gunboats. All day and all evening, more and more troop-ships had been congregating at Mudros; surely the Turks must know of the preparations, and would evacuate the hills and plains of Gallipoli rather than face the inevitable massacre? Many of the strangely archaic Greek fishing boats, which slipped into the harbour between the black transports, were thought to carry Turkish spies: news must have travelled across the fifty-mile stretch of sea, Patrick thought. But, whether or not the Turks knew of it in advance, the plan could hardly fail. Landings were planned at several beaches simultaneously, with fake attacks on the Asian side of the peninsula to dilute enemy resistance. The Battalion Commander, who had addressed the Epping Foresters before they embarked, had predicted an easy victory.

"This is the finest body of men it has ever been my privilege to send into battle. I am confident that the Gallipoli landings will be recorded in the regimental history as a testament to the courage and discipline of the Epping Foresters . . ."

History in the making, Patrick thought, and he would be here to see it, take part in it . . .

The lighter, with several others, was approaching the troop-carrier, so that Patrick could see, above the bulk of her hull, the forecastle padded round with sandbags and converted into a makeshift gun-turret. The River Clyde was an unlikely Trojan horse. She was a coal-ship, battered and grimy next to the immaculate Navy men-of-war, like a dray-horse lining up with elegant thoroughbreds at Newmarket or Ascot. She would have been more at home in the industrial riverways of Europe than here in Homer's Aegean . . .

"Not the most cushy way to travel," Allington said drily, eyeing the coal-blackened hull. "For real luxury you want to end up on that hospital ship, that huge one. Converted from a first-class passenger cruiser, Wingfield told me. Wouldn't be a bad way to get home."

Patrick thought of the hospital ship lying empty of patients, the beds waiting to be filled. It was an ominous thought.

"I'd prefer not, all the same."

He turned his attention to the collier. To adapt her for her new role, huge sally ports had been cut into her sides so that the disembarking troops could run straight out to the bridge of smaller boats which would take them to the shore. In just a few hours' time . . . The landings would be the first

step towards an Allied victory, the master-stroke
which would open up the gateway to Constantinople
and the Caspian Sea, and knock Turkey out of the
war: Winston Churchill's inspired plan to break the
deadlock on the Western Front. Patrick's awe was
mixed with a heavy sense of the responsibility of
leading his platoon into action for the first time.
He hoped he would not let himself down – let
them down. His was a regular battalion, not a
new one formed of Kitchener volunteers, and he
felt appallingly young and inexperienced when he
compared himself to the non-commissioned officers,
some of them seasoned from tours in India or even
the Boer War. He felt sure that the fifteen private
soldiers he was supposed to be commanding were
well aware of his inadequacy. In this respect, he felt
that Edward had fared better, having being put in
charge of a platoon of new recruits in a Kitchener
battalion.

Patrick remembered the letter to Edward in his
pocket, half-finished, and felt it superstitiously
through the fabric of his jacket, wondering what
he would have to report next time he had a chance to
write. If only Edward could have been here, standing
next to him instead of the stolid and unimaginative
Allington . . .

The lighter was coming alongside the River Clyde,
converging with another craft carrying Dublin Fusiliers. Patrick's ears tuned to familiar accents as the
Irish troops called to each other and prepared to
board the troop-ship. With only a small change of
circumstances, he would have been over there with
them . . . He heard his own name shouted, and
looked round to see who had called before realising

that there must be dozens of men in the Dubliners who shared it. But the voice shouted again, urgent and familiar.

"Padraig! *Padraig!*"

There was only one person who used his name the Gaelic way. He looked across at the mass of khaki in the other craft and saw a figure thrusting through to the side of the lighter, elbowing others out of the way.

"Brendan!" he shouted back. "I'd no idea you were out here!"

"You should have got yourself into a decent regiment," Brendan yelled, already further away; the two boats were divided by a widening stretch of churned water as the craft carrying the Foresters pulled further along the side of the troopship. Brendan was slipping out of view, still shouting, "See you on board, or on the top of Achi Baba! We'll be there before you . . ."

His voice was drowned by shouts of "Up the Dubliners!" and Patrick lost sight of him amidst upraised arms and waving caps.

Allington had watched the incident with wry amusement. "One of your Sinn Fein comrades?" he suggested.

Patrick ignored the taunt. "He's my cousin."

"I bet you wish you were over there with him, eh? Fighting for the glory of Ireland?"

On board the River Clyde, there was nothing to do but wait. Some of the men were dozing where they sat, but Patrick felt too excited to sleep, too crowded in amongst other men to sketch, or continue writing his letter to Edward. He wished he could have found Brendan; a good talk would have passed the hours very satisfactorily, but with two thousand troops on board there wasn't a hope in hell of finding him, to say nothing of the impossibility of clambering over the equipment and sprawled sleeping men taking up every inch of floor space in the hold. How odd to think that he and Brendan were virtually together after all, here on the same ship . . . he thought of Edward, still, as far as he knew, stuck in training camp. Edward would feel left out when he got the letter, envious of his two friends. By the time he wrote it, Patrick thought, he would be on Gallipoli; he would have seen some real action instead of just running over taped lines on the ground. The enemy would be real, not just sacks of straw. He wondered whether he would have to kill another man, face to face. He did not want to contemplate it. It was easier to think of the enemy.

It was getting increasingly stuffy in the packed hold, smelling of sweat and coal. Allington mumbled in his sleep. Dawn could not be more than an hour or two away, Patrick thought, shifting cramped limbs. His stomach felt queasy, not with seasickness but with fear, reminding him incongruously of the first time he had gone in to bat for the junior cricket eleven. He told himself that the comparison was ridiculous, but couldn't help feeling comforted by the fact that he had scored a creditable twenty-two not out . . .

His thoughts were interrupted by an explosive crash in the distance. The sleeping men muttered and stirred. At first Patrick mistook it for thunder, but he corrected himself quickly: of course, it was the start of the artillery barrage from the navy gunships. For an hour before dawn, shells and mortars would pound the coastline. The Turks, if they'd any sense, would have retreated to the safety of the hilltops long before now, Patrick thought. He pictured the invading troops stumbling over smashed dugouts, fragments of rock and timber . . . and corpses? He would not think of that. The barrage increased in intensity, shells screaming overhead until the whole ship seemed to reverberate with the shock waves. Everyone was attentive now, blear-eyed faces abruptly jolted into alertness. Rations were passed round, but Patrick's stomach was churning too much to allow him to think of eating anything. The ship must be close to V-Beach, ramming her prow as far forward as she could; the navy cutters would be towing the lighters round to form the bridge to the shore, across which the Dubliners would soon be leading the assault. Patrick thought of Brendan, somewhere on the ship, tensed, ready . . . confident, expectant, frightened? He would be one of the first to get to the beach, to storm the ruined castle at Sudd-el-Bahr and on up the rocky slopes from which Allied troops would soon command the whole peninsula . . .

It was time to get ready. Sergeants chivvied those who were slow to get to their feet. Most of A and B Company were already standing, taut-faced.

"Don't look so glum, lads. We'll be sunbathing on the beach in a few hours," a man called Stringer, a Lance-Corporal, shouted above the din.

His attempt at levity was met with a few half-hearted grins. No-one else was in the mood for joking. Patrick saw the men in his platoon exchange anxious glances as the roar and crash dwindled. The contrasting silence was so sudden that it seemed to exert a painful pressure on his eardrums.

"Fix bayonets," the order came. Patrick looked round at his platoon to check that they had all heard. The Foresters began to move into position by the nearest sally port. Patrick, whistle in one hand, revolver in the other, shifted his weight to each foot in turn. It would almost be a relief to get moving at last, to burst out of the ship into the cool dawn air . . .

It was time. The exit ramp was lowered, and A-Company ahead moved into position on the threshold. The high-pitched, nerve-jangling whine of a shell ripped the air, and spume sprayed up as the missile plunged into the sea. A second shell clanged against the side of the ship, making the nearest men scrabble away in panic. The Turks were firing back . . . but they should have been obliterated . . . lining up with B-Company, Patrick heard, above the noise of explosions, the screams of men from the cutters. The Dubliners should be ashore by now . . .

No time to think; Captain Wingfield signalled to Patrick and the other officers and they were surging forward, out into the dawn, not rosy-fingered as Homer had seen it, but filled with screams and acrid cordite-smelling smoke. Patrick expected to see lines of troops ahead running across the bridge of boats and fanning out across the beach. Instead, he saw only chaos: the air seemed to be thick with zinging lead, like enraged hornets . . . and the Dubliners ahead were not making orderly progress to the beach, but dying. They fell to bursts of machine-gun fire or toppled headlong into the churned sea, the water already stained red with great dark clouds of blood.

Mother of God, it's suicide to go on . . .

Brendan . . . BRENDAN . . .

His legs were weak with the shock of seeing what he had just seen. He forced himself to go forward, certain that he would be killed before reaching the shore. There was no choice, orders must be obeyed come what may; if your orders were to die, you must die obediently . . . Men were falling all around him, throwing up their arms as they flopped back, collapsing across the bridgeway, clutching at wounds, mouths wide in agonised screams. There was no possibility of stopping; those behind clambered over them and staggered on. They were like targets at a fairground shooting booth, Patrick thought, easy prey for the concealed Turkish snipers and machine-gunners. He felt the rush of air as bullets passed close to him, and the scream of shells whizzing overhead . . . he kept his head down and ran on. His feet skidded and slithered under him and he looked down to see dull red coating the wooden deck . . . Someone ahead turned to shout something incomprehensible, his face contorted into a snarl. The shore was a few yards ahead now; a handful of men had made it to the beach, while the sea was clotted with tangled khaki, a thick soup of dead and dying men. Patrick's frantic gaze took in the curve of the coastline, the squat castle of Sudd-el-Bahr, as described, and the fissured hills rising behind . . . There were screams from the water, and he saw the coils of barbed wire in the shallows, trapping men who had tried to wade ashore and were now being picked off by the snipers.

A rifle cracked like a whip and he saw one of the men jerk back, the sinews of his neck straining, face up to the sky as if he had been socked on the chin by a prizefighter . . . The man's body spreadeagled into the water and sank from view, giving Patrick time to see the face, and the torn scarlet hole in the chest . . .

. . . *Brendan* . . .

Patrick stopped, rigid with shock. Someone cannoned into him and cursed: "Get on with it, you silly bastard." The pressure of men from behind forced him to move forward, stifling his urge to dive into the sea, certain that it had been Brendan he saw but wanting to confirm it . . . Brendan was dead, his numb brain registered . . . they would all be dead within minutes . . . but he was making progress, the shore was only yards away, and he flung himself from the final section of the boat-bridge to sprawl in pebbles and sand. Another man thudded into him from behind and he picked himself up as the remnants of his platoon scuttled across the last stretch and jumped ashore or flopped into the shallow water. The beach had seemed a hundred miles away when he had been on the lighters, but it was no safe haven . . . Those who had survived so far were crouched together in a slight dip in the sand, as helpless as penned sheep encircled by wolves. Some of the men were firing back wildly, firing at nothing but rocks and scrub where the Turks lay concealed. Patrick felt a bullet rip through the sleeve of his tunic, and he clasped his arm to feel the trickle of blood where it had grazed the skin.

An officer from the Munsters was trying to take

charge. "Get down, find some cover, here, dig in, dig in –"

Patrick looked around wildly for any senior officer from his own battalion. Dig in, here, with the bullets thudding and zipping all around, sending up fountains of sand and pebbles . . . ? His own instinct was to lead what was left of his platoon into the shallow sandhills, where there was more natural cover . . .

Someone else was shouting defiance. "We can't last out here, sir, let's get the men back to the boats . . ."

"Impossible," the Munster captain bawled back. "Get the entrenching tools out, damn it . . ."

Patrick heard the burst of machine-gun fire before it hit him. The force of it threw him backwards . . . tearing, burning, like flaming swords disembowelling him . . . He rolled over, squirming like a speared fish, clutching at his stomach. His face was in the sand, there was blood in his mouth and in his throat, but he was horribly conscious, not dead as he surely ought to be . . . A scream of pain was choked off into a gargle in his throat . . . He would die soon, he could not be so violently wounded and still live . . .

The voices continued to float around him. "Help that man, someone . . ."

"No time for that – dig in, for Christ's sake, before we're shot to pieces . . ."

He must be going to die. Someone should shoot him in the head, like an injured horse, put him out of his misery . . .

Going Back

"Patrick! Are you all right?"

His eyes focused slowly on Edward's face, which loomed at him like something in a dream. The Gallipoli beach, the sounds of gunshot and shell and screams, were more vividly present to him than his real surroundings. He closed his eyes and swallowed hard, and the vision faded. But the curtain had lifted, finally, he knew. He remembered clearly what had happened on the first day of the Gallipoli landings.

"Brendan's dead," he said dully.

Edward looked at him in bafflement. "Yes, I know. That's what I was trying to tell you. But I thought you already knew."

"I must have known all the time. Oh, God." He felt like weeping, faint with delayed shock.

"You're ill. Let me fetch a nurse –"

"There's no point," Patrick protested weakly. But Edward was already on his feet, dodging a group of slow-moving elderly visitors. He approached the Staff Nurse, who was assisting a man on crutches. Patrick heard his voice raised in urgent request.

"My friend – Lieutenant Leary – he's ill, having

hallucinations or something. Can you come and do something for him?"

The Staff Nurse looked at him pityingly and then across at Patrick.

"Nothing I can do about that, I'm afraid. He isn't the only one. He'll get over it."

"I'm all right. Really I am," Patrick tried to assure Edward as he came back to the bedside and sat down rather hopelessly.

"You don't look it."

Patrick felt that he must gather his wits together, more for Edward's sake than for his own; Edward seemed more upset by his peculiar mental condition than he was himself.

"About Brendan," he said shakily. "How long ago did you hear about it?"

"In June," Edward said. "I didn't see his name in the casualty lists, but Mary wrote to me."

"Poor Mary. Poor all of them."

"Yes."

One day, Patrick thought, he would tell Edward everything he had remembered, but not now; the memories were like newly-opened sores, raw and painful. There was silence for a few moments, each absorbed in his own thoughts. Then the gong sounded for the end of visiting time, and the friends and relatives of patients began to filter slowly out of the ward. Edward got up to go, reluctantly.

"I'll write as soon as I can."

"Yes. I'll write too. And – good luck."

Superstitiously, Patrick watched for the last glimpse of Edward as he paused in the ward entrance and then passed out of sight down the corridor outside.

His last impression was of Edward's pale, taut face, forcing a smile as he looked back.

His memories of the catastrophic Gallipoli landing, returning with such force and immediacy, refused to go away. Each time he fell into a doze he saw Brendan, the taut arc of his body lurching back from the bullet's impact, the ragged scarlet hole in the chest, the body sinking into the churned water . . . In his dream, Patrick tried to move towards him but his feet dragged as if he were moving through thick treacle, and he could do nothing but watch as the body subsided, the wound in the chest slowly releasing a thick dark stain into the water. The face was momentarily visible in a grimace of death, the blurred features sometimes resolving clearly into Brendan's, sometimes superimposed with Edward's anxious white face . . .

Brendan could not have died there in the turbulent waves . . . It was Edward who had nearly drowned, and Brendan who had saved him . . .

Each day Patrick expected his father to appear, but each day he was disappointed. He had written a long letter home, and was beginning to worry that there had been no response. Perhaps his father had been taken ill, he thought; but if that were the case, he would have expected some sort of reply to his letter, a brief note at the least.

Three days after Edward's visit, Patrick, scanning the visitors anxiously as usual as they entered the ward, recognised a tall well-dressed lady who was making her way purposefully towards him, bearing a huge sheaf of Michaelmas daisies.

"Aunt Constance!"

She bent to kiss him, engulfing him in a drift of lavender perfume. "Dear boy. How good to see you safe, if not well. You've grown up a lot since I last saw you, I will say."

Patrick smiled. "Well, it must be three or four years after all. You haven't changed at all, yourself!"

"I wish I could agree. I'm beginning to feel my age."

Aunt Constance was ten years older than her brother, Patrick's father. She looked rather like him, sharing his height and imposing bearing. She must be approaching sixty, Patrick supposed, but her years did not diminish the force of her presence. She was immaculately dressed, from shining buttoned boots to a beige felt hat decorated with bronze fabric flowers. Answering her questions about his health, Patrick thought of a Christmas at her house shortly after his mother had died, their first Christmas without her. He remembered the warm, enveloping comfort of the Hampstead house as something from a previous life, his pre-war life. He wondered how she had known where to find him, and, more importantly, whether she had any news of his father.

"I've written home," he said, "but Father hasn't replied, or been in to see me. Have you heard from him at all? I hope he's not ill."

"That's why I've come, dear. He's staying with me in Hampstead, after having bad back trouble in the summer. We only knew you'd arrived in London when the letter was forwarded. Your father's had to shut up the Epping house; he couldn't have managed there without a nurse, not at first. He's still not

84

fit enough to leave the house – otherwise he'd be here now."

"Will he get better?"

"The doctor thinks so, but it will take time and rest. There seems little point in him going back to Epping until he's fully recovered. I think he finds it lonely in that big house by himself."

"Yes," Patrick said, with a twinge of remorse.

"He sends you his love, of course, and he'll visit you as soon as he can. You heard about Brendan, poor young fellow?"

Patrick agreed, not going into any detail.

"Your Uncle James has taken it very badly. The whole family has, needless to say, but James in particular. He didn't want Brendan to enlist – they had quite an argument about it, I heard. He would have preferred Brendan to join the Citizen Army or the Volunteers."

"I was surprised, in a way, that Brendan was so keen," Patrick said. "He always seemed to be an ardent nationalist. He would have been quite justified in having nothing to do with the war."

"I hope he didn't have time to regret his decision," Aunt Constance said. "At times like this you only get one choice."

"I don't think he could have regretted it," Patrick said slowly. "It was all so sudden – the way the landings went wrong. I saw him just a few hours before and he looked very cheerful."

He hoped his aunt wouldn't question him further, but she just nodded thoughtfully and said no more. He wondered what her attitude would have been if she'd had a son of her own. Like his father, she had left Ireland but still had nationalist hankerings,

85

particularly since her English husband had died. When Ireland's problems were finally resolved, Patrick thought, it wouldn't be at all surprising if all of them – his father, his aunt and himself – went back to Dublin.

"Your father's concerned about what will happen to you when you're fit to leave hospital," Aunt Constance said. "I suppose you'll be sent to convalescent hospital when you leave here, but after that? You won't be fit for active service again?"

"The Medical Officer thinks it's possible after all. I've made a better recovery than they though at first. But it won't be for a good long while. I'll have a long convalescence and then go before a Medical Board when the time comes," Patrick said, aware for the first time that with the Epping house closed up he would have nowhere to go. He had been in the army for little more than a year, but already the thought of being out of it while the war was still in progress made him feel aimless.

It was as his aunt guessed his thoughts. "You'd be very welcome to come and stay with me and your father."

"It's kind of you. Thank you very much," Patrick said. "I shall have to think carefully what to do."

"Anyway, from the look of you," Aunt Constance said, "you won't need to decide anything just yet."

Patrick realised that he ought to write to his Dublin relatives, to tell them of the circumstances of Brendan's death. It was a difficult letter to compose, but he was thankful that he was able to tell them, truthfully, that Brendan had been killed instantly, and had not suffered the agony of a long drawn-out death. The knowledge would give them some small comfort, he hoped.

A week later he received a letter from Aunt Margaret in reply.

"We were so sorry to hear that you are wounded," she wrote, "but praise be that you are out of this awful war. Constance has written to us about your father, and with the house in Epping being closed up we wonder whether you would like to come and stay with us here as soon as you are fit enough to travel. It is a very sad time for us all of course, but we would all love to have you for as long as you wish."

Patrick, struck by the possibility, read the letter through several times. Why not go to Ireland? It was certainly a more attractive prospect than staying in war-weary London. He already knew that he wanted to go back there after the war. Why not get acclimatised now? His thoughts ran ahead. Dublin; walks in the Wicklow Hills when he was fit enough; his young cousins for company . . .

He got out his pen and writing-paper and began writing a reply to Aunt Margaret.

PART TWO

DUBLIN,
SPRING 1916

Cousins

The last time Patrick had visited his aunt and uncle's house in Rathmines had been three years earlier, before the war had been thought of. He was a little disconcerted, on arrival, to be shown by Mary to Brendan's room. On the wall was a framed photograph of Brendan, Edward and himself, taken on that previous visit: Brendan was standing behind the garden bench on which the other two sat, leaning forward with his arms round their shoulders. All three were smiling broadly, eyes narrowed against the sun.

Mary saw the direction of Patrick's gaze and said, "I hope you won't mind. Being in this room, I mean. We could have put you in with Cathal, but . . . and Mother says we can't keep this room shut up for ever."

"I don't mind," Patrick said. He didn't think it would make much difference which room he was in. The house was haunted anyway, with Brendan's and Edward's ghosts everywhere he looked. He had to remind himself that Edward wasn't dead. Since the long illness and death of his mother when he was twelve, he had a deep-seated and often irrational fear that people close to him would be abruptly taken away. Since the beginning of the war, that fear had begun to seem more justified.

Mary looked at the photograph intently, her large eyes shining with tears. Patrick was afraid that she would cry, and was not sure what he would do if she did, but after a few moments she turned to him, brightening, and said, "It's grand to have you here, Patrick. I've been so looking forward to it."

"So have I." He was uncomfortably aware that he seemed to have achieved wounded hero status in her view, a role which he neither wanted nor deserved. The frank admiration in her eyes made him feel self-conscious and foolish. He would tell her soon, he decided, that he had done absolutely nothing in the war except get himself shot within minutes of going into action for the first time. The role of hero would prove difficult to live up to.

"I hope you've got everything you need," she said, straightening the edge of the candlewick bedspread.

"Thank you. It's good to be in a proper house again, with a room to myself, after all those months of being in hospital."

"I know. You've had to put up with so much. It must have been terrible for you."

She put her hand on his arm and looked up at him with such overflowing sympathy that he said, more brusquely than he had intended, "Not really. Convalescent hospital was quite cushy. What I've missed most since joining the army is privacy – there's never a chance to be on your own when you've had enough of other people."

The words were hardly out of his mouth before

he realised that she might interpret them as a hint that he wanted her to leave him alone. Her tender expression faded, replaced with something more guarded. She took her hand away. "Yes, it must be annoying," she said, turning slightly away from him. "Well, I'll leave you to unpack your things. Come down when you're ready and I'll have some tea made."

She left the room quickly, and Patrick cursed himself for being tactless. She had always been sensitive, he remembered, doting on her brothers and himself and Edward, wanting nothing more than to please them in every way she could, and deeply wounded by every imagined slight. He should have been more careful, knowing that her emotions were still raw from the death of her brother.

He unpacked his few belongings and hung his clothes in the wardrobe, which had been cleared of Brendan's garments. Apart from that, the room was just as Brendan had left it: his books were on the shelves, there were some school certificates pinned above the fireplace, and a clumsily-fashioned clay horse pranced on the mantelpiece. Patrick moved to the window to look out at the rain-washed garden. On the wall beside the wardrobe, mounted and framed, was the little drawing he had done of Edward and Brendan arguing. He felt rather touched that Brendan had kept it so carefully. He looked at it critically, noticing that for all the roughness and haste of the execution he had succeeded in catching a likeness of both his subjects. It was a while since he'd done any drawing, and it occurred to him that it would be a very suitable pastime now, while he had time to spare during the few remaining weeks of convalescence.

Suddenly conscious of how tired he was after the journey, he resisted an urge to lie down and sleep, remembering that Mary and Aunt Margaret would be waiting for him in the drawing-room. He washed his face and hands at the basin, combed his hair and went downstairs.

The house was quiet. Cathal was out somewhere, and Uncle James, after a brief greeting, had gone back up to his attic studio. He seemed, as usual, preoccupied with his work, and Patrick guessed that his response to his son's death had been to absorb himself in his painting. He had become a well-known portrait painter in the last few years, attracting regular commissions and high fees, while his wife took care of the business side of things.

Aunt Margaret seemed as sane and well-balanced as ever; the grief she undoubtedly felt for her son, Patrick thought, was not allowed to show. Over tea she questioned him about his army experiences and travels. He was glad that she didn't ask him directly about the Gallipoli landings, sparing him the ordeal of going over it all again. Mary presided at the tea-table, darting in and out with fresh hot water and more scones, foreseeing everything Patrick or her mother might want. She seemed to have taken over a good deal of the running of the house, now that her mother was otherwise occupied. Patrick wondered whether she would always find this as satisfying as she appeared to at present; surely, at her age, she would rather be setting up a home of her own? She was twenty-two, two years older than Patrick, quite old enough to be married. He found himself observing her closely as she moved around the room refilling tea-cups and passing the sugar bowl. She was shorter than her mother, with a stocky figure like Brendan's; she would probably put on weight as she got older. Patrick had to admit, for all his fondness for her, that she was plain; her thick, soft brown hair was her best feature, but she had not inherited her mother's austere good looks. She was so obviously cut out by temperament to be a wife and mother that he thought it a pity she was still single. He could easily picture her with a large brood of children.

"I'm so glad to hear that your father's improved," Aunt Margaret said. "We were worried about him. And how's Edward getting on? Have you heard from him recently?"

Patrick saw Mary look up quickly.

"I haven't seen him since the autumn, when he visited me in hospital," he said. "And he sent me a short note recently from the front. He wasn't able to say where, of course."

He wondered how Mary would react if she knew about Edward's affection for the unknown Alice. Probably, with her overwhelming generosity, she would be pleased for him, even though Patrick suspected that she had had romantic yearnings for Edward herself. The feeling had been entirely one-way; Edward had been unfailingly courteous and considerate towards Mary, but would, Patrick felt sure, have been amazed to learn that she felt anything more than friendliness towards him.

He didn't meet Cathal until the next day. His younger cousin was still out when the rest of the family went to bed; Patrick was surprised by

Aunt Margaret's vagueness as to his whereabouts, but remembered that she had always allowed her children – the boys, at any rate – more freedom than was usual.

Patrick heard footsteps mounting the stairs some while after he had gone to bed, followed by the closing of the bedroom door next to his own. He slept heavily, tired out by the long day of travel, and by the time he went downstairs in the morning Cathal had left to catch the bus to his school in Rathfarnham.

In the afternoon, Mary and Patrick went out for a short walk, and when they returned there was a school bag and coat dumped in the hallway.

"Oh – Cathal's home," Mary said. Her voice betrayed the tension Patrick had noticed when she had spoken of her brother the day before.

The creak of floorboards above suggested that Cathal was in his room.

"I expect he's just gone up to change," Mary said. "He'll come down and see you in a while. Let me make us all some tea."

She waved aside Patrick's offer of help, and sent him into the drawing-room, where Aunt Margaret was working out her household accounts. Cathal came down a few minutes later; he clomped down the stairs and was apparently on his way out of the front door again. Aunt Margaret, hearing, called out, "Cathal! Patrick's here. Come in and say hello!"

The boy who reluctantly entered the room was very different from the shy twelve-year-old of three years earlier. He had shot up in height, with the lankiness of adolescence, and was only an inch or two shorter than Patrick, who stood up to greet him. He had untidy fair hair, and a thin face, with deep-set light-brown eyes, the same colour as Brendan's. He wore an outdoor coat and muffler over his brown jacket and trousers.

"It's good to see you again, Cathal," Patrick said.

"Hello." Cathal shook Patrick's hand briefly, unsmiling.

"Won't you have some tea?" Mary asked her brother. "It's freshly made."

Cathal shook his head. "No, thank you. I'm going to Michael's. I don't know what time I'll be back."

"What about – ?" Mary began, but Cathal was already in the hallway putting on his coat. Mary hurried after him and could be heard asking whether he would back for supper; Cathal said that he didn't think so, and went out, almost slamming the door behind him.

Aunt Margaret gave an apologetic shrug. "I'm sorry about my son. He's rather difficult just now."

"I hope he doesn't mind my being here," Patrick said.

"Oh no, not at all." Aunt Margaret's reply came too readily to be convincing. "He's still very upset about Brendan. Particularly because Brendan died fighting for the British army. He's developed strong nationalist views lately. Of course, we wanted to encourage that – that's why we sent him to Mr Pearse's school – but with the war, and Brendan in the army, and now the talk of conscription, it's all becoming very difficult. And then there's the problem of his schooling. St. Enda's seems to be in trouble – financially, I mean, with the enormous upkeep of the house and grounds. Cathal will be heartbroken if we have to move him to another school. There just *isn't* another school like St. Enda's, and he adores Mr Pearse."

"Yes," Patrick said. "I remember last time, when we saw him in the pageant."

Aunt Margaret gave him a sidelong glance. "He's changed a lot since then."

"He has," Patrick agreed. The cousin he had just met was hardly recognisable as the enthusiastic youngster of two years ago. Cathal's manner reminded him, more than anything, of Brendan, when Edward had come to stay for the first time. Brendan, he reminded himself, had thawed; perhaps Cathal would. The loss of a brother must be very difficult to bear, particularly at his impressionable age. And Brendan's presence was almost tangible in the house, as if his personality were too strong to be obliterated by the mere accident of death.

Looking across the room, he realised that he was sitting in the same chair he had sat in to draw the caricature, and for a moment his memory recreated the sound of voices raised in dispute, Brendan's and Edward's.

"No, no, you don't understand at all –"

"If you'd just let me answer –"

Patrick listened helplessly as his cousin and his friend argued hotly. It was so stupid – if only Brendan would be quiet and listen for a moment, he'd realise that Edward actually agreed with him in principle. Brendan was arguing with his idea

98

of a typical Englishman, rather than with the real person. And Edward, who had refused to be drawn into open argument until now, was becoming increasingly impatient with him.

" . . . and you really expect us to be content with Home Rule," Brendan stated, as accusingly as if Edward were personally responsible, "after all the persecution over the centuries? One of the richest countries in the world – *your* country – let a million Irish people starve without lifting a finger to do anything about it –"

"England may be my country, but that doesn't mean I'm proud of everything she's ever done, or ever will do –"

" – and then fobs us off with Home Rule, and thinks we'll be grateful for it? Still part of the British Empire – and that's only if the government turns out to be gracious enough to give us even that much – Do you really think it's enough?"

"No, I *don't*," Edward said emphatically, having been trying to make this point heard for the last few minutes. "But if Ulster won't agree to Home Rule, how likely is she to accept total independence?"

"Ulster will have to put up with it, you said so yourself . . ."

"Home Rule will satisfy most Irish people for the present, and give a better basis for negotiation in the future. It's a first step, that's all I'm trying to say . . ."

Patrick, who had joined in the discussion at first, now found that he couldn't get a word in. He looked at the other two across the room. Edward sat on the sofa, Brendan on a low chair; as the argument had gathered momentum, they had moved closer together, both leaning forward with their elbows on their knees. Patrick suddenly noticed how comically similar they looked in profile, shoulders hunched, chins jutting, eyes narrowed in determination. He picked up his drawing pad and soft pencil from the table and began sketching rapidly, with deft, sure strokes, eager to catch the pose. Caricature was not his preferred style of drawing, but it had earned him popularity during his school years, and he had had enough practice to capture a quick likeness. A few short stubby lines for Brendan's hair, a thick swirly scribble for Edward's; he bent closer over the pad, concentrating on the finishing details of clothing. He thought of drawing in speech balloons issuing from the mouths . . .

"Padraig! What are you doing?"

"Wait, I haven't finished yet . . ."

But Brendan crossed the room and snatched the pad, ignoring Patrick's protests. He frowned at the drawing for a moment, and then gave a shout of delighted laughter. "Padraig, you devil! Edward, will you take a look at this now . . ."

Edward, who had been the victim of Patrick's pencil before and knew what to expect, took the sketch with a grin already spreading across his face. "Never trust Pat when he's got a pencil in his hand," he said to Brendan. "He's notorious for it."

"Well, I should know that well enough." Brendan shook his head slowly as he looked at the drawing once more. "You ought to do this sort of thing for the newspapers, Padraig. Perhaps Father's got a rival in the family with artistic talent."

"Don't be stupid. It doesn't take much talent to

do that sort of thing. Not as much as Uncle James has got in his little finger." Patrick reached out to take the pad back, but Brendan said, "Will you let me keep it?"

"Yes, of course, if you want it," Patrick said, pleased that his small diversion seemed to have created some sort of harmony between his cousin and Edward.

"Have you done any drawing since you've been in hospital, Patrick?" Aunt Margaret asked, as if she could read his thoughts by following the direction of his gaze. "You used to be so good at it."

"No, I haven't. I was just thinking I'd like to start again. I'll need to get myself some pencils and paper."

. . . What had happened to the drawings he had done out in Egypt? . . .

"I'm sure James could give you something," his aunt said. "I'll go up and ask him in a moment. If not, you could go to the art suppliers' with him and buy what you need. I think he said he was going tomorrow. He's run out of Viridian Green, or something equally vital."

Patrick thanked her, and then excused himself and went up to his room to fetch the book he was reading. He stopped to look again at the framed caricature. It would have been difficult at that moment, he thought, to predict that Edward and Brendan would become close friends. Brendan's automatic resentment and Edward's unintentional air of superiority had not been a promising combination . . .

It had taken time, he remembered, for Edward to reveal that he had just the same doubts and frailties as anyone else.

Brendan suggested that they all three went out riding in the Dublin mountains; he had a friend in Stepaside who would let them hire horses. Patrick agreed at once, but to his surprise Edward hesitated and said, "I'm afraid I'm no horseman."

Brendan's eyebrows shot up. "You must be able to ride, surely?"

He had probably classified Edward as the typical young English country gentleman, Patrick thought with amusement, a hard rider to hounds.

"I've never ridden in my life. Not unless you count once on the beach at Southend, on a Shetland pony, when I was about five."

"You often drive your father's pony-trap," Patrick said.

"Yes, but riding's different. You have to actually sit on the animal."

"Well, you may as well start now," Brendan said cheerfully. "Tom's sure to have some quiet old nag you can amble about on."

They set out for Stepaside on bicycles, after Edward had been persuaded that he wouldn't spoil the outing for the other two. Brendan's acquaintance, Tom, was a small man in his fifties or sixties, some sort of dealer, with an assortment of horses and ponies housed in various ramshackle outbuildings and paddocks. He produced two hunter types for Patrick and Brendan, and then brought out an enormous Irish draught horse for Edward.

Edward stepped back in alarm. "I'm not getting

on that huge creature. Haven't you got something more like a Shetland pony?"

"He'll not hurt you, sorr. He'll look after you like a mother with a new baby, so he will." To demonstrate the horse's placidity, Tom ducked underneath its stomach and then walked round behind and swung on its tail.

"Go on, Edward. You won't find a quieter horse," Brendan urged. "We'll be lucky if we get him out of a walk."

"We'll make sure you're all right," Patrick said, from the back of his own mount. He couldn't help being amused by Edward's open admission of nervousness; it was a completely unfamiliar side of him.

"Well, if you're sure," Edward said doubtfully.

Tom led the horse over to a mounting-block and Edward scrambled into the saddle, where he sat awkwardly while Tom adjusted the reins and stirrups. The horse was wearing a double bridle, and Edward managed to get the two sets of reins in loops and tangles like someone trying to skein wool for the first time. When he was finally ready, Brendan led the way out of the yard, and the three horses made their way along the lane and up a forest track towards the hills. Patrick, who wouldn't have been in the least surprised if Edward had turned out to be a gifted natural rider, soon saw that this wasn't the case; Edward simply didn't look right on a horse.

"I feel ridiculous, perched up here," Edward called out.

"You look ridiculous," Patrick confirmed.

"Won't I hold you up, while you witch the world with noble horsemanship?"

"We'll go on ahead in a minute, and you can catch up at your own speed," Brendan told him.

Edward feigned terror. "You're not going to leave me alone with this savage beast?"

"Afraid so," Brendan said heartlessly, and as soon as the track opened out on to a grassy plain he and Patrick urged their willing horses into a headlong gallop, hurtling up the gradual incline towards a low summit. The horses raced, their hooves throwing up clods of dusty earth. Patrick's horse was keen, its stride long and free, as if it would keep going into the misty purple distances. His spirits surged with the exhilaration of speed; it was a long time since he'd ridden, too long . . . He was no expert, and rode with more energy than style, but well enough to enjoy himself.

"Don't forget about Edward," Brendan shouted. The horse he rode was beginning to tire, its neck patched darkly with sweat. Patrick pulled back to a canter and the horses mounted the final rise and slowed to a halt, their sides heaving. The two boys grinned at each other with the satisfaction of the gallop, letting their horses rest and stretch their necks. They had risen far enough above the larch and spruce plantation to look down on Dublin and the Liffey estuary, blurred in the haze of the summer day. Palls of smoke from factory chimneys hung above the city, like grey veils. Beyond, the oddly-shaped Howth peninsula jutted out into the sea, making Patrick remember his childish game of finding pictures in atlases; on the map, the peninsula was like a sea lion's flipper.

"It looks smaller from here than you'd think, Dublin," he said.

"Baile atha Cliath," Brendan corrected. "Why use the English name?"

"Pedant. We use English names for everything. Neither of us speaks more than the odd word of Irish."

"No. More's the pity. Cathal does, though – they teach it at his school. Lucky little gossoon, having Patrick Pearse for a headmaster. I ought to make the effort to learn it myself. How can I call myself a real Irishman when I don't speak my own language?" Brendan turned in his saddle to look back in the direction they had come, and gave a snort of laughter. "Will you look at this?"

Edward, still some distance down the track, had managed to get his docile horse into a plodding trot. He was making erratic progress. When, after every few yards, the horse slowed to a walk, Edward urged it faster with flailing legs and waving arms, and then clutched wildly at its mane as it lurched into a trot again. He was red-faced with effort by the time he reached the others. When the horse put its head down to graze, he slumped over the front of the saddle, arms dangling.

"You didn't tell me it was so exhausting," he mumbled. "I thought the horse was supposed to do at least some of the work."

Patrick, unable to help laughing, said encouragingly, "We'll stay together from now on. Then it'll be easier to keep your nag going."

Now, four years later, Patrick could still recall his sense of acute disappointment.

In spite of his teasing, he hadn't liked to see his friend in such an undignified role; he had never before discovered anything Edward wasn't good at. Edward's ready acknowledgement of inadequacy where horses were concerned should, he supposed, have reassured him; like everyone else, Edward found some things daunting and difficult. But Patrick wasn't at all sure that he wouldn't have preferred to keep his illusion intact.

"The irony of it," Uncle James said, "is that if there had been conscription in 1914 – even a hint of it – Brendan would never have enlisted. He would have gone to prison rather than give in to compulsion. The whole point of it was that he enlisted of his own free will. Ireland's not included in the Conscription Act now, but if they try to bring us into it again it'll raise the seven devils. The British government doesn't seem to know how to accept a free gift. They wouldn't even let us have our own Irish Brigade."

Patrick leaned over the parapet and watched the brownish waters of the River Liffey flow past. The characteristic Dublin smell of malt and yeast from the Guinness brewery was strong in his nostrils, and a dray loaded with barrels passed by on the opposite side of the river. It was all so familiar that he could hardly believe that he had been to Gallipoli and back since the last time he had stood here.

"I'm not really sure why Brendan did decide to enlist," he said, cautiously, as he knew that it was a touchy subject.

Uncle James sighed heavily and turned, leaning his back on the stone wall. "I suppose, like many people – yourself too, probably – he thought it was his duty to help Belgium, a small vulnerable country. And that if we offered help to England in her hour of need, she'd be obliged to repay us with Home Rule after the war."

"But Brendan wouldn't have been satisfied with Home Rule," Patrick said. "He told me so, time and time again."

"I know." Uncle James' gaze followed the flight of a herring gull which balanced effortlessly on the air-current over the river. He had the same iron-grey hair and stern features as Patrick's Aunt Constance, but was more bohemian in dress, wearing now, as usual, a brown velvet jacket, floppy bow tie and an ancient felt hat. He had the same light-brown eyes as the rest of the family, in his case hooded by heavy lids, giving him a brooding expression. He continued, "Probably, like a lot of young men, he was inspired by the enthusiasm of the moment. Expecting a quick victory, and a blow struck for Irish nationalism. No-one could have guessed that the war would drag on for so long, and still no victory in sight after nearly two years. That fool Redmond sold Irish lives for the mere promise of Home Rule – with partition as part of the parcel."

"Will it come to a division of Ireland, do you think, after the war?" Patrick asked.

"It's the only way Carson and the Ulster loyalists are going to accept Home Rule. And of course it's not a solution at all. But that's what we'll get. Unless something drastic happens meanwhile."

Patrick looked back along the river in the direction of Liberty Hall, where they had just stopped to look at the banner boldly displayed across the frontage: WE SERVE NEITHER KING NOR KAISER, BUT IRELAND.

"England's difficulty is Ireland's opportunity," Patrick murmured. "All these rumours of an insurrection – do you think they'll ever come to anything?"

"Those rumours have been flying around since the beginning of the war," Uncle James said cryptically. He pulled his watch out of his waistcoat pocket and consulted it. "Come on then, let's walk along to the art suppliers', or they'll be closed for lunch."

Uniforms

Mary took it upon herself to ensure that Patrick took the prescribed walk every afternoon, planning a different route each day. Her concern varied between a wish for him to build up his strength, and anxiety that she was overtiring him, in spite of his protests that he felt perfectly all right. Often, for variety, they would take a tram to the city centre and walk back. Spring was advancing; the silhouettes of trees in the parks were misted with new foliage, and there were budding lilacs and daffodils in some of the city squares. There were troops everywhere. Officers on leave sat in the pubs and cafes or strolled about the streets, mingling with convalescent soldiers dressed in distinctive blue. Patrick had been issued in hospital with a blue uniform of his own, worn with a white shirt and a red tie, but he had discarded it since arriving in Dublin in favour of his own clothes, even though he suspected that Mary would prefer to be seen out walking with a young man clearly identifiable as a wounded soldier rather than as a possible shirker. For himself, he preferred the anonymity of civilian clothes, and felt that his recovery was so far advanced that he would feel a fraud in convalescent uniform.

There were other uniforms besides those of the British army to be seen on the streets and squares of Dublin. One afternoon, walking back from St. Stephen's Green, Patrick and Mary came across a marching column dressed in the grey-green of the Irish Volunteers. Patrick saw with surprise that the men carried rifles.

"Doesn't the Castle do anything to stop them?" he wondered, thinking of the rumours.

Mary was dismissive. "They never do anything except parade about, them and the Citizen Army. I think the Castle thinks they may as well be allowed to play their silly games if they've nothing better to do. It's a fine thing to be playing at war when there's a real war on. Fit young men, like most of those are, ought to be ashamed of themselves. No-one takes much notice of them."

She certainly didn't share the nationalist fervour of her father and brother, Patrick noted.

"So you don't think there'll be a rebellion?" he asked her.

She gave a derisive humph. "If they dared try it, they'd soon see what they were up against. It might knock a bit of sense into them. But all they're good for is talking about it." She slipped her arm through his. "Even with the way it turned out, I'm proud of Brendan for doing what he did. He wouldn't have been Brendan if he'd stayed at home. I'm proud of the both of you."

She looked up at him adoringly, making him feel like a great fool. He felt that he ought to discourage such an attitude, but wasn't sure how to. After all, it wasn't surprising if she wanted to treat him as a substitute brother for a while.

"I've to call in at the shop on the way back," Mary continued, holding his arm more tightly as they crossed the low humped bridge over the canal. "I forgot to put down coffee in this week's order."

"Felihy's?" Patrick asked, remembering the corner shop where he and Brendan used to buy peppermints and chocolate.

"No, didn't you know? The Felihys sold up about four years ago and moved out of town. There's another family there now, the MacBrides. They must have been here last time you came, but you probably didn't go to the shop."

The shop had been enlarged since Patrick's last purchase there, and had widened the range of its stock. The interior smelled warmly of fresh bread from ovens at the back, and there was a large counter of cheeses and meats; shelves reaching from floor to ceiling displayed tinned goods, preserves, jars of coloured sweets, coffee in plain cloth bags and tea in printed packets and enamelled tins. Patrick, remembering Aunt Margaret's special liking for ginger marmalade, asked an assistant if he had any. By the time the boy had found it behind the apricot jam on the bottom shelf, Mary was engrossed in conversation with a dark-haired girl who had emerged from the rear of the shop with an armful of fresh loaves.

When Patrick had paid for the marmalade, Mary said, "Come over here and be introduced. This is Siobhan MacBride. Siobhan, this is my cousin Patrick. He's staying with us while he's convalescing."

"Are you in the army?" the girl asked.

"He was wounded in the fighting at Gallipoli," Mary said proudly, before Patrick could answer.

"Is that so?" The girl looked at Patrick with increased interest. "I've a brother-in-law in the Fusiliers, but he's still here in barracks."

Patrick, aware that Mary's comment had given a misleading impression, and about to explain that he was not in an Irish regiment but an English one, was relieved when Mary spoke again, saving him the trouble.

"Bridget's coming to tea on Saturday. I was wondering would you like to come too. We could have a proper talk."

"I'd like that," Siobhan said, "if I can get Michael to take my place here for an hour or so."

Mary completed her purchases, and as she and Patrick walked home she explained, "Bridget – the older sister – is my closest friend, but I don't see her so much now. She moved away to Terenure when she was married. And the younger brother, Michael, is Cathal's friend. Siobhan's the clever one of the family."

"How many are there?" Patrick asked.

"There's Donal, the eldest, he's about twenty-three. He hasn't enlisted – not in the army that is. He was more than likely in that bunch of toy soldiers we saw earlier on. Then Bridget, she's my age. Siobhan must be eighteen, and then there's Michael, who's the same age as Cathal. And a younger girl, Roisin, about fourteen or fifteen. I used to think," she said wistfully, "that Brendan was sweet on Siobhan."

Patrick stored away this new piece of information: something else he hadn't known about Brendan. For some reason, it had never occurred to him that there was room in Brendan's life for girls.

At home, he took his new sketch-pad and pencils into the drawing-room and got to work on the drawing he had already started. He had decided to do a portrait of Mary, which he thought would please her. At first he had asked her to sit for him, but she wasn't very good at posing, self-consciously arranging her features into what she took to be a suitable expression. Patrick, wanting a less contrived result, found it more useful to steal glances at her when she thought he wasn't looking; he had made a number of quick sketches, which he used as reference for the portrait when Mary wasn't around. If it turned out well, he thought, he would frame it and give it to her. He knew that she had already been painted a number of times, far more skilfully, by her father, but he wanted to give her something in return for the time and attention she was lavishing on him.

While he drew and frowned, rubbed out and drew, he found himself thinking again of what she had told him earlier. He was aware for the first time that both his closest friends, Brendan and Edward, seemed to have ventured into romance, something which his own life so far had lacked. School, his limited social life in Epping, and then his brief period of army training and service, had provided him with few close female acquaintances. He had met girls who seemed pleasant and friendly, but had had neither the inclination nor the opportunity to follow up any of these encounters. Brendan and Edward clearly had, against the odds in both cases: Edward was involved with someone of a different social class, and Brendan seemed to have been fond of a girl from, Patrick assumed, a Catholic family. Would this have caused problems, if Brendan had survived? – Patrick held the drawing at arm's length, scrutinised it and then rubbed out all that he had just drawn in; it was so difficult to get the eyes to look in exactly the same direction . . .

He heard the door creak open behind him, and Cathal came in and looked at the drawing over his shoulder.

"The nose is too long," he said.

Patrick looked critically at the drawing again.

"It's difficult to tell with only one eye properly drawn, but I think you're right."

"The rest of it's quite good though," Cathal said. "I like the way you've done the hair. You've made her look prettier than she really is."

Patrick looked towards the open doorway, hoping that Mary wasn't within earshot.

"I don't think so," he said. "But I'm glad you like the hair. It isn't very easy."

"I can't draw at all. Everyone expects me to be able to, being my father's son. Brendan couldn't, either."

Patrick continued working on the awkward eye. This was already the longest conversation he had had with Cathal, and his cousin seemed prepared, for the first time, to be friendly.

"I expect you're good at other things," he said.

"Oh yes, I am." Cathal smiled rather secretively, not elaborating. Patrick hoped his remark hadn't sounded patronising, the sort of thing you might say to someone much younger. He did not want Cathal to think he was condescending to him.

Cathal watched him draw in silence for a few minutes, and then asked abruptly, "Did you like being in the army?"

"There wasn't much time to like or dislike it," Patrick said. "I was just there, like everyone else."

Cathal took off his school coat and flung it over the back of the sofa, and loosened his tie. "If the war goes on for another three years, I shall be old enough to enlist. But I never will, not even if they bring in conscription. *Especially* not if they do."

"I hope it's a decision you don't have to face."

"You mean if the war ends before I'm old enough?" Cathal's tone was ironic. "It won't make such a lot of difference. There's still a war going on in Ireland. I shall still have to fight for one side or the other. And I already know which."

"Do you think Brendan did the wrong thing, then, joining up?"

"No. I know why he did it." Cathal leaned against the backrest of the sofa, closing his eyes.

"Why, then?"

"He wanted to get a proper military training. To learn how to use a rifle and a bayonet, and about bombs and machine guns. So that after the war he'd be a trained soldier, ready to train others. He wouldn't wear British army uniform for any other reason."

"I see," Patrick said carefully, not sure what reaction Cathal intended to provoke.

"But," Cathal continued, "he isn't here, and you are." He suddenly opened his eyes very wide and stared at Patrick, still leaning back on the sofa.

Patrick stared back. "What do you mean by that? You're not suggesting –? In any case, I shall have to go back to my regiment. As soon as I pass a Medical Board, and that won't be much longer. It's not my choice to make."

Cathal nodded slowly, as if he had known what to expect all along. "It *is* your choice. It's just easier to pretend you don't have one. But it's just as I told Mother. You call yourself Irish," he went on, his voice hardening, so that he sounded like someone much older, "but you're really a West Briton. You know which side you're on."

At that moment, before Patrick had time to retaliate, Aunt Margaret walked into the room, seemed mildly surprised to see her son and nephew talking together, and looked at Patrick's drawing. "Oh, that is a good likeness of Mary," she remarked. "Isn't that funny? James never found her very easy to paint. Do you always work in pencil?"

While she was speaking, Cathal picked up his coat and slipped out of the room. Patrick thought it was just as well his aunt had come in at that point in the conversation; he would have found it difficult not to rise angrily to the bait dangled before him, which he was sure had been Cathal's intention. He chatted to his aunt, and carried on drawing, half his mind on what Cathal had just said. The motives Cathal had ascribed to his brother were certainly plausible, perhaps more so than Uncle James' somewhat vague interpretation. And in saying, "He isn't here, and you are," had Cathal merely been stating a fact, or seriously suggesting that Patrick should carry out the role Brendan had planned for himself? Leave the army, and go with his military knowledge to the Citizen Army or the Irish Volunteers? Support the more extreme nationalist minority in an armed rebellion against the British forces? If Cathal had meant it, it showed how little he understood. The Conscription Act had already come into force in England, and as an officer in an English regiment Patrick would certainly be expected – compelled, if necessary – to report for duty as soon as he was fit. Cathal was just a schoolboy, he told himself, probably repeating things he had heard in rumours, imitating his brother's attitudes: impressed by the romantic notion of defying the British in arms. And yet there was something cynical and knowing in Cathal's manner which made it impossible to dismiss him as a mere schoolboy, young though he was.

Cathal was badly mistaken in another respect too, Patrick thought, recalling his cousin's final accusation. Patrick did not know which side he was on. The more he thought about it, the more he concluded that his loyalties lay with both sides at once.

Once, after a debate at school, the classmate who had been proposing the motion which Patrick was supposed to support had said to him, "I'm not debating on your side again, Paddy. Never mind what the topic is."

"Why? Was I that bad?" Patrick had said, hurt.

"Your trouble is, you're too good at seeing everybody else's point of view. Sometimes you need to stand up for your own."

He thought of this as he stood by his bedroom window looking out into the darkness. A fine rain was falling, so that the garden breathed out scents of damp earth and fresh greenery; he could hear the soft splash, hardly more than a whisper, of the raindrops on the leaves of the rowan tree below his window.

117

Above the thick shrubbery of the garden he could see dim lights from other houses beyond, in another street. Dublin. Ireland. People in England talked of Ireland and the Irish as if the country had a sort of collective will, as if the attitude of all the people who lived their various lives, whether comfortable or wretched, contented or resentful, could be lumped together in one convenient category. Far from being able to judge what the people of a whole country thought about the Irish Question, Patrick realised, you couldn't even guarantee that the members of one family would be in accord with each other. There was Uncle James, with his interest in the Gaelic League, an Irish Irelander for all that he was a descendant of the Anglo-Irish ascendancy; Aunt Margaret, who seemed to accept a range of attitudes without much curiosity; Mary's unquestioning support of British supremacy; Cathal's fierce nationalism. And Brendan.

Patrick finished washing and got into bed. He propped up the pillows, leaving the light switched on. He was lying in Brendan's bed, in Brendan's room, looking at Brendan's books and belongings. He had heard, by now, several different opinions about Brendan from the various members of the family. How much had any of them really known?

Patrick felt newly conscious of his own ambivalent position. He considered himself Irish and a patriot, but he was also, in a way, English and a patriot. At the outbreak of war he had automatically considered it his duty to fight for England against German oppression. He had assumed that when Home Rule was granted after the war, Ireland's problems would be over. Now it seemed that England would extract

118

advance payment in the form of thousands of Irish dead, their lives squandered in the trenches of Flanders and on the beaches of Gallipoli. And the final reward would be a divided Ireland, a betrayal of the ideals of all the old dead Fenians who had fought and died for independence. Home Rule would be as Brendan had described it, a sop, a discarded bone tossed to a dog to keep it quiet. It was easy enough to personify England as the harsh persecutor of Ireland throughout its long and tragic history. And yet England was not an abstract collection of evil attributes, just as Ireland could not be pinned down; it was, Patrick thought, the gently undulating countryside at home, and school, and the forest and Bell Common, and Edward.

His meditations seemed to have got him nowhere. He was still no clearer as to where he stood. But he must have been prepared to die for England; shouldn't he, logically, be as willing to die for Ireland, his own country? Yet that was too simple a comparison. Dying for England was straightforward enough – you simply enlisted and were sent to some front or other where you would be shot at or shelled. The idea of dying for Ireland was far more complicated.

Remembering that he had not cleaned his teeth, he got out of bed and reached for his toothbrush, catching sight as he did so of his reflection in the oval mahogany-framed mirror above the washbasin. Sometimes, as now, he felt surprised when he saw his own face. It was reasonable enough as faces went, somewhat broad, with regular features dominated by strongly-marked dark eyebrows and deeply-set brown eyes. It was the expression which surprised him; it seemed to be the face of someone older, more confident, even more virile, than he felt. Perhaps one day he would grow into it, but for the moment he felt that if he attempted a self-portrait it would be a stranger's face he drew.

Undertow

"I must call in at MacBrides to remind Siobhan about Saturday and see whether she'll come," Mary told Patrick as they set out to catch the tram into the city.

Siobhan MacBride was not serving in the shop today; instead, a stocky-figured woman in a white apron and cap stood behind the counter, accompanied by a younger girl of about fifteen.

"Good afternoon, Mrs MacBride. Hello, Roisin," Mary greeted them. "It's a fine day."

"'Tis all that. What can I be getting for you?"

"I don't need anything today, thank you. I came in to see if Siobhan was here."

"She's upstairs, reading away at her books. I'll call her for you."

Mrs MacBride pushed through the bead curtain which divided the shop from the family's living accommodation. Throughout the brief conversation, and while her mother was gone, the girl, Roisin, stared at Patrick with unabashed curiosity, one little finger curled into the corner of her mouth. He noticed at once that she was quite beautiful, with long dark hair, and a sort of unselfconscious animal grace. His artist's eye saw and approved, while another part of him was faintly disturbed by the combination of childishness and physical maturity. He wondered how the masculine-featured Mrs MacBride could have produced such a daughter.

A quick rush of footsteps down wooden stairs preceded the arrival of Siobhan, who greeted Mary and Patrick and said, "I hadn't forgotten about Saturday. The only thing is I may be a little late. I've to go to the Castle at two o'clock."

"The Castle?" Mary echoed.

"Yes," Siobhan said with evident pride. "I'm to be interviewed for Red Cross work."

"A nurse?"

"No. Ambulance driver."

Mary looked amazed. "Sure, I didn't know you could drive."

"Jimmy Shanahan's been teaching me in the fish van." She smiled. "Everyone's been complaining about the smell of my clothes."

Her air of determination reminded Patrick of Edward's sister, Lorna, who had never allowed mere practical difficulties to stop her from doing what she wanted. He remembered that Mary had described Siobhan as the clever one of the family, and he asked her about this as they walked to the tram.

"Yes, she wants to get a place at the National University," Mary said. "It's hard for her, not coming from what you'd call an educated family. I think her mother's rather expecting that she won't manage it. She'd rather see her settled, like Bridget."

"It must be difficult for a girl," Patrick said. He supposed that for most girls the range of choice was really very limited: get married, or stay at home, or else take some low-paid job. He was about to say that for a lot of girls the war had brought new opportunities for travel and independence, but stopped himself from mentioning it in case Mary thought he was criticising her. It was too easy to upset Mary.

His dream came back to him that night. He was standing watching while Brendan sank slowly into the bloodstained sea. He knew that he had to plunge in and haul Brendan out before he drowned, but something was preventing him: fear, like some unseen heavy thing clinging to his limbs . . . The sea boiled up and then the waves retreated, pulling with them the clotted khaki mass of human jetsam, and then Brendan was gone . . . there was just a blood-smear on the sand to show where he had been. And then the face came back, a tragic, dead face, reproaching him . . . Brendan's face, bloodied like Banquo's ghost . . . Edward's face . . .

He woke up in a tangle of bedclothes. He felt hot and sticky with sweat; the details of the dream were so sharp in his mind that it was a few moments before he remembered that he was in Brendan's room, in his aunt and uncle's house. Stripping off his pyjama jacket, he got out of bed and went to the washbasin where he washed his face and hands and then splashed cold water over himself.

Why did he keep imagining that Edward was dead?

He went to the window and looked out at the garden, breathing the cool air and thinking about the various elements of the dream. It was a relief to realise that he had been confusing two quite separate episodes, not receiving some telepathic message from Edward at the front. He was thinking of the holiday at Ballyteige Bay three summers ago, Edward's second visit to Ireland. The family had rented a cottage on the south coast by the beach. Patrick remembered floating on his back, looking up at the blue sky and thinking about dolphins while Edward nearly drowned.

The water lapped at him, tugging gently at his hair, occasionally washing over his sun-warmed face so that he felt the sneezy taste of salt in his mouth. It was like lying on a floating cushion, the cool swell buoying him up. The sigh of the waves against the pebbles of the beach was a long way off. From time to time he raised his head and made small paddling movements to stop himself from drifting out too far. Cathal, who had tired of swimming, was walking slowly along the beach, head down, probably looking for scallop shells. Between Patrick and the shore, though still in deep water, were Edward's and Brendan's bobbing heads; he could hear them shouting to each other. Mary usually protested to Patrick if she saw him swim out so far, even though she knew he was the strongest swimmer of the four boys, but he could see that she was almost out of sight, just the top of her head visible in the dunes where they had had their picnic earlier.

He liked to think of the depths beneath him, of the unseen life of the sea. He wondered if there were dolphins along this stretch of the coast; he had always wanted to see a dolphin. He had read stories of them playing with swimmers and following boats, as if they sought human company. The ancient Greeks knew about dolphins, how they would come to the rescue of a drowning human, pushing the body up to the surface or even back to the safety of other humans or a ship. How did they know? Did they pick up telepathic signals of distress, or was it merely chance, that they saw the floating object as a toy to be played with and pushed to the shore? And if you were out in the sea, a shipwrecked sailor, perhaps, and a dolphin tried to rescue you, would you realise what it was trying to do? Patrick imagined the cool smooth touch of it under the water, pushing and lifting him. You might easily panic, thinking it was a whale or a shark attacking you . . .

He lifted his head suddenly and listened, alerted by an urgent shout. Looking towards the shore, he saw that there was only one bobbing head where there had been two.

"*Edward* . . . Edward . . ." He heard the catch in Brendan's voice as if he had swallowed a mouthful of sea-water, and before that, the note of panic.

Where was Edward . . . The water seemed suddenly cold, threatening. Patrick struck off as fast as he could towards the place where Edward had been. He was a powerful swimmer, but the sea seemed to be opposing him, diminishing his efforts, pushing him back from the shore so that the distance between him and the shore seemed stretched like elastic . . . the sea, which had seemed so benign a few moments ago, was fighting him, an enemy . . . his arms and legs ached, his heart would burst with the effort, while Edward drowned, out of sight . . . Ahead of him Brendan was swimming in frantic circles, his head swivelling in every direction. Cathal, on the

125

beach, had seen what was happening and ran into the shallows, fell over, struggled up again, and pointed at something, yelling. And then, while Patrick was still too far out to do anything to help, Brendan launched himself forward and up-ended himself, legs thrashing the surface, and disappeared from view. Swimming more slowly now with his head above water, Patrick fixed his eyes on the spot in case Brendan failed to reappear. A minute . . . how long could you hold your breath under water? And then a head broke the surface, Brendan's, streaming and spluttering, and he was pulling something with him, a limp shape, Edward, dragging him towards the shallows. Patrick, his feet touching sand at last, raced to help him, and between them they hauled Edward to the shoreline and laid him on the sand like a basking seal.

"Quick, turn him over, face down . . ."

"Give him artificial respiration, someone . . . Doesn't anyone know how to do it?"

"Oh Jesus, Mary and Joseph, he's dead . . ."

"Shut *up*, Cathal . . . he isn't . . . his eyes moved . . ."

"Fetch Mother . . ."

And then Edward raised his head slightly and spluttered, and a trickle of frothy water ran out of his mouth on to the sand. He turned his head and his eyes opened briefly, brilliant as a Siamese cat's against the bedraggled black of his hair and his bluish-white skin. He was breathing, with short shallow breaths at first, then with great frightened gulps as if the air rushed into him of its own accord. The colour slowly flushed back into his cheeks.

"God Almighty . . ." Brendan looked as if he

were almost weeping with tension and relief, but practicalities took over. "Padraig, rub his hands, get his circulation going . . . Cathal, run and get one of the blankets, will you, or the towels . . ."

The boy hovered. "Is he going to be all right?"

"Edward, are you all right?"

Edward slowly got his breathing under control, and then he propped himself up on one elbow and said, "I'm perfectly all right, thank you," with such polite formality that Patrick and Brendan exchanged grins of immeasurable relief. And then Mary and Aunt Margaret and Uncle James were running towards them from the dunes, their feet slithering and crunching on the pebbles.

"What's *happened*?"

"Get him further up the beach . . ."

"*Edward* . . . Oh Patrick, I said you shouldn't swim out so far! Mother, didn't I say to you, Patrick swims out too far . . . Edward, thank God . . ."

"But it wasn't Patrick who —"

"Brendan, you were heroic . . ."

"Why did you let him out of your *sight*? I told you to be careful . . ."

"I only turned away for a minute or two and when I looked back he'd vanished."

"I'm terribly sorry to be such a nuisance."

"Oh, don't be such a bloody idiot . . ."

"I had a sudden cramp in my leg . . . I just slipped under the water somehow . . . and then I couldn't seem to get to the surface."

"By the mercy of God, Cathal spotted him."

"Just a glimpse – I thought I saw something under the water, that was all . . ."

"Look," Uncle James said firmly, "don't you

think all the explanations should wait until we've got the poor boy dry and warm?"

"Of course," Mary exclaimed. "What are we thinking of? Get him up to the dunes and we'll bring the blankets. We've got some hot tea left in the flasks . . ."

The night air was cold, stirring the curtains. Patrick shivered and got back slowly into bed, rearranging the disturbed sheets and pulling them up over his shoulders.

He remembered how bitterly he had reproached himself while Edward was plied with blankets and towels and tea and sympathy. He had been uselessly daydreaming about dolphins and shipwrecked sailors while a few hundred yards away Edward had nearly drowned in the cold choky depths. He had let him slip, out of his reach, beyond his help.

Mary's tea-party was on Saturday. Bridget MacBride arrived early, with her two small children; she was clearly expecting another fairly soon. Patrick, having now seen all three MacBride sisters, thought how very different they were from each other. Bridget, of the three, was the most like the mother, he thought: although only twenty-two or three, she was plump and matronly in appearance. The two children clung to her skirt at first and looked up at Patrick and Aunt Margaret with large, wary eyes. Mary clearly adored them, scooping them up into her arms and pressing her cheek to their flushed faces; Patrick thought that she probably envied Bridget. Bridget's husband, he gathered from the fragments of talk, was in the Dublin Fusiliers, and was garrisoned at the Portobello Barracks close by. It was not easy to carry on a conversation, though, as the children gained confidence in their new surroundings and began to roam around the room, picking up books and ornaments.

"He looks like being in Dublin for another two months at the least – put that down, Daniel, be a good boy now . . . So you were in the Dardanelles, Patrick, did I hear Mary say – Bridie, no, that's someone's drawing-book, don't be creasing the pages . . ."

Patrick, not used to young children, thought Bridget's two were like small boisterous animals. They took little notice of their mother's admonitions, and he was relieved when Aunt Margaret found them an ancient picture book of Cathal's and sat them down on the sofa, one each side of her. At that point Siobhan arrived. She sat down in the the empty chair next to Patrick's, and gratefully took the cup of tea Mary poured for her.

"That tastes good. I'm quite parched. They kept me waiting for nearly an hour in the Castle and then there was such a queue for the tram that I walked all the way back."

"But what about your interview?" Mary asked. "Did they take you on?"

"They did. I start at the beginning of Easter week."

"So you'll get your training as a driver?" Patrick asked her.

"Yes, and not just driving, but vehicle maintenance as well, changing wheels and all that sort of thing. Perhaps I'll end up getting a job as a garage hand!"

"You won't be needing to do that, Siobhan, will

you?" Bridget said. "Not with the other ideas you have for yourself."

There was an edge of resentment to her voice, and Patrick saw that in spite of the friendly way in which the sisters had greeted each other there were undercurrents of hostility. He looked from one to the other. They seemed to be as unalike in temperament as they were physically; Siobhan, unlike her mother and two sisters, was small in build, with neat regular features and lively dark eyes which seemed to observe everything in the room. She had none of the languid, almost insolent beauty of her younger sister, but seemed characterised instead by restless energy. She sat perched on the edge of her chair as if she could spare only a few minutes for the visit; this, with the thinness of her wrists which protruded from the frayed cuffs of her jacket, made her seem birdlike. Her appearance made it difficult to imagine her changing a punctured tyre by a roadside. But, Patrick realised, her frail exterior must conceal a tough and determined personality. Although he had hardly spoken to her, he had formed the impression that she was someone who knew what she wanted in life, and was likely to get it.

He felt interested by what he had seen of the MacBride family. And there was still the older brother Mary had mentioned, the one who was in the Volunteers. Surely there must be conflicts there, he thought, with Bridget's husband in the army and Siobhan about to start work for the Red Cross . . .

Mary handed round plates of sandwiches and fruit-cake. Siobhan ate delicately but quickly, putting away considerably more of Mary's sandwiches and fruit-cake than Patrick felt able to manage. Bridget began telling Mary in a low voice about a funeral she had been to, and Aunt Margaret continued reading aloud to the children, leaving Siobhan and Patrick to make conversation together. Patrick was about to ask her about her intention of applying for a place at the National University, but she spoke first.

"Was it as disastrous as everyone says, out in the Dardanelles?"

Patrick wished he had got out his own question more quickly.

"From what I saw at first hand, it was. It certainly wasn't what we'd been told to expect. But I really didn't see very much."

"But you must have heard a lot more about it from other patients in the hospital?"

"Well, yes . . ."

She asked him a great many questions about his experiences, revealing detailed knowledge which she must have picked up, he supposed, from the newspapers.

"Does anyone know where Cathal is this afternoon?" Aunt Margaret asked suddenly, closing her book. "I thought he'd have been here by now."

"I think he's at the shop," Siobhan said. "Michael said he'd help mother this afternoon, and I think I heard him say that Cathal was coming round."

Aunt Margaret nodded, looking rather displeased. It was obvious to everyone in the family that Cathal avoided being in the house as much as possible while Patrick was there.

"So the two younger brothers are friendly, as well?" Patrick asked Siobhan.

She looked at him sharply. "As well as what?"

Patrick realised that he had been indirectly alluding to her association with Brendan, and that as she had not mentioned the subject herself she might not want it to be generally known.

"As well as the other friendships between the families, I meant," he said lamely.

"It's quite possible for Catholics and Protestants to be friends," she said, misunderstanding. "Do you find that surprising?"

"Of course not. I mean . . . we're not exactly devout Protestants, I'm not at any rate, and I don't think Brendan was . . ."

"Brendan?" She seemed surprised. "Oh no, Brendan wasn't. I don't think he was particularly interested in religion. He wasn't the sort of nationalist who saw it as tied up with Catholicism. He wanted an independent Ireland for Catholics and Protestants alike."

"Not everyone sees it like that, though. Not in Ulster."

"Home Rule will be Rome Rule," Siobhan quoted. "Religion often gets in the way of things, doesn't it? I didn't really know Brendan all that well," she continued. "He came over to our house often, but that was usually to see my older brother, Donal."

"Oh – I see." It was Patrick's turn to be surprised. "Your brother who's in the Irish Volunteers?"

"Yes." She paused for a moment, then said abruptly, "Do you disapprove? You're in the British army, after all."

"So was Brendan. Did he disapprove?"

She smiled, as if acknowledging that he had scored

a good point, then said: "But you haven't answered my question."

They had instinctively lowered their voices, not wanting what they said to be heard by the others. Patrick suddenly realised that Mary and Bridget had stopped talking and were looking curiously in their direction.

"What are you two whispering about?" Bridget sounded suspicious.

"We were just talking about Brendan," Siobhan said lightly. She stood up. "Well, I must be getting along home. Thank you very much for inviting me, Mary."

Patrick received a letter from his father.

" . . . *I am feeling very much better, and now that summer is appraching I shall go back home to Epping and open up the house. Aunt Constance has offered to come and stay with me there for a week or two until I have hired a new housekeeper. She has been most kind, but nevertheless I am looking forward to being back in my own house. It will be a relief to me to know that you have some-where to stay on leave when you have rejoined your regiment.*

I was very pleased to receive your letters, and am glad to know that you are progressing well. I shall look forward to seeing you in a month or so; write to me at home."

"Father says he's much better," Patrick said to Aunt Margaret and Mary across the breakfast table. "He's going back to Epping."

"Oh, I am glad," his aunt said. "That will be such a relief to us all. He's always been so independent that it was hard to think of him as an invalid. And it will be nicer for you when you go back."

"It will."

Patrick saw Mary's troubled expression as she rose to clear away the dishes.

"Oh, Patrick, I wish you didn't have to go," she burst out. "I hate to think of you going back to that terrible war."

He smiled at her and said, "Well, it's your fault after all. All that walking you've made me do. I shall be fighting fit by the time I go to the Medical Board."

His teasing remark fell flat. Mary gathered up a pile of dishes and fled into the kitchen, looking stricken. Patrick, exchanging rueful glances with his aunt, wondered whether to go after her.

"She'll miss you when you're gone," Aunt Margaret said.

Patrick nodded. "I shall miss her – all of you."

When he had arrived in Ireland, the time in front of him had seemed to stretch hazily to some unseen horizon, like desert sands. Now the sand had shrunk to a measurable quantity, trickling too quickly through an hour-glass. His remaining time could be calculated in days, not weeks. He knew he would be passed fit by the Medical Board; the ugly scars across his lower abdomen would be his permanent legacy of the Gallipoli landings, but otherwise he had made a full recovery. He would be sent to training camp, and then, he supposed, to the Western Front. The Dardanelles campaign had ended in failure and the opposing armies in France and Belgium were locked into the stalemate of trench warfare. Cuinchy, Béthune, La Bassée . . . the names, familiar from army conversations and news articles, would soon turn into reality, while Dublin and its tensions would fade into something he read about in the newspapers.

A Picnic at Howth

"But it always rains at Howth."

"Oh, do stop grumbling, Cathal," Mary said. "If it's raining on Saturday morning then I'm sure we won't go."

"I don't want to go anyway. What's the point in traipsing all the way to Howth to have a picnic in the rain?"

"But it's for Michael's birthday. I thought you'd have been pleased to be asked."

Cathal stood at the window looking gloomily out at the twilit street. "If it's for Michael's birthday then I don't see why a whole crowd of people has got to go."

"It isn't a whole crowd of people. It's the MacBrides and you and me and Patrick."

"It's raining now." Cathal turned to face the room with an expression of triumph. "It's bound to rain on Saturday. And anyway, who's looking after the MacBrides' shop? Why don't I stay behind and do that?"

Mary cut off a length of cotton and threaded her needle with a brisk practised gesture. "You shouldn't be so ungrateful to Siobhan. And she's already said that Donal will mind the shop."

"I'll mind the shop instead then, and Donal can go to Howth."

"Siobhan's invited you because Michael would want you to be there. But if you're going to do nothing but complain then I'm sure we'd all prefer it if you did stay behind."

"You sound just like a governess."

"Well, and you're behaving like a spoilt child after all."

Cathal glowered at his sister, strode out of the room and clumped noisily upstairs. Patrick had had enough. He knew the real reason for Cathal's objection. He climbed the stairs two at a time and caught up with his cousin in the doorway to his room.

"Would you stay out of my bedroom?" Cathal said sharply, trying to close the door in his face.

Patrick placed himself just inside the door, wedging it open.

"Look, Cathal, you've got to stop behaving like this. Can't you see you're upsetting Mary?"

Cathal's face was flushed with indignation. "Didn't I tell you to get out of my room?"

"Yes, but I'm not going to. Not until we've sorted this out."

"There's nothing to sort out." Cathal's eyes were almost on a level with Patrick's as he faced him defiantly.

"Yes there is. It's nothing to me whether you like me or not, and I shall be leaving anyway in less than three weeks. But I do mind that you're being selfish and unreasonable and making things difficult. All that nonsense about the weather and minding the shop – can't you just agree to go on this picnic to please Siobhan and Michael and Mary?"

"Mary won't mind whether I go or not," Cathal flashed back. "Not as long as you're there."

Patrick was momentarily taken aback. Cathal had a way of undermining him, aiming straight for his weaknesses.

"That's rubbish," he retorted. "She just wants you to make an effort for once. Mother of God, it's not such a punishment, is it, to have to go on your friend's birthday picnic?"

"Mother of God," Cathal mocked. "Why do you talk like an Irishman, when we all know you're an Englishman underneath?"

Patrick, his anger roused by his cousin's sneering tone, moved a step closer. Cathal didn't back away, but for a second Patrick saw his defiance waver, as if he feared a physical assault. Controlling the urge to grab him and shake some sense into him, Patrick said quietly, "I'd be a bit more careful what you say in future. You can think what you like, but don't dare to say anything like that to me again. You don't even have to speak to me at the picnic if you don't want to, but you *do* have to go and you do have to be pleasant to everyone else. Now I want you to go downstairs in a minute or two and tell Mary you'll go. Will you do it?"

The unintentional threat of intimidation had had its effect. Cathal turned and sat down sullenly on his bed, avoiding looking at Patrick. He said indistinctly, "Oh, all right. If you're going to make such a fuss about it."

After such an unpromising beginning, Patrick was pleased when he got up on Saturday morning

138

to see that the weather looked reasonable. It had rained earlier, but the sun was shining through breeze-scattered clouds and the sky was fresh blue beyond. Like a blackbird's egg, Edward had once described it on a similar day. No, Patrick corrected himself as he took a clean shirt from the wardrobe, it had been the other way round – Edward had said that a clutch of blackbird's eggs they had found in the forest were like pieces of sky . . . He wondered where Edward was now, and tried to dismiss his feeling of guilt at setting out on a family picnic while Edward was probably brewing up tea in a dugout in some squalid front-line trench. Edward's last letter had come from Béthune.

The party – a large group, consisting of Patrick, his aunt and his two cousins in addition to the whole MacBride family apart from Donal – made its way out to Howth by tram and train. They carried numerous baskets and hampers as far as the steeply-climbing cliff path, where they settled for the picnic among flowering gorse bushes on a slope overlooking the harbour and the small rocky island called Ireland's Eye. A fresh breeze from the sea made them keep their coats on, but there was no sign of the rain which Cathal had confidently predicted. Patrick, looking at his cousin where he sat a little apart from the group with his friend Michael, was relieved that he had apparently resigned himself to the outing and even seemed to be enjoying himself, eating ravenously and joining in when Michael's health was toasted in lemonade and ginger beer. Siobhan had made a birthday cake which Mary had decorated in pink and white icing, and when this had been cut up and eaten the two boys said that they were going down to look at the harbour.

"Let me come too," Roisin said, standing up.

Michael, a very quiet thin-faced boy, said, "No. We don't want you with us."

"Oh, *please*. Cathal, you don't mind if I come, do you?" Roisin looked at Cathal with a pleading expression. Had Cathal been a few years older he would have found it hard to resist, Patrick thought, but he shook his head and said, "We've got something we need to talk about in private."

"You can come down to the harbour with us a bit later on, Roisin," Mary said soothingly, and Roisin sat down again disconsolately on one of the spread blankets, next to Siobhan. Patrick, who had brought his sketch book and pencils, considered doing a sketch of the two girls side by side. He looked at them speculatively, realising that a joint portrait would show Siobhan at a disadvantage, completely eclipsed by her younger sister. And then Roisin got up again almost straight away and said that she would take Bridget's children for a walk up to Howth Head.

"It'll be too far for them," Bridget said.

"Well, we'll see how far we can get."

Relieved of the children, Bridget, Mary and Mrs MacBride were soon engrossed in conversation, and Patrick thought he might go down and do some sketching at the harbour. However, when he had helped to put the picnic things away, Siobhan said quietly, "Would you come for a walk with me? I need to ask you about something."

"Yes, of course," he said, surprised.

They began to retrace their steps down the cliff

path towards the harbour, walking slowly so as not to catch up with the two boys. Siobhan said nothing at first, and Patrick wondered what she could want to discuss with him. Something she could not talk about in front of the others, presumably – something about Brendan? But she had said that she didn't know Brendan particularly well, that he had been more friendly with her elder brother . . . Patrick was beginning to feel curious about Donal, the only one of the MacBrides he hadn't met. He wondered whether Siobhan's decision to work for the Red Cross had caused friction in the family; to Donal, a member of the Irish Volunteers, it might be the same in effect as joining the British Army . . .

"It's on Monday you start your Red Cross work?" he asked Siobhan.

She was walking slightly ahead of him on the narrow path. "It is," she said. "I shall go to London later in the summer when I'm trained. And if the war carries on I hope to get out to France."

"And your place at the National University?"

"That will have to wait until the end of the war. I haven't got a place even – I mightn't get one at all. It's difficult enough. I've been trying to educate myself to the entry standard. But they won't take me seriously at home. They think it's something I shall grow out of."

"But it isn't. I hope you succeed."

Siobhan looked out at the sea beyond the harbour, her dark eyes narrowed against the brightness. "I *will* succeed. I have to. If I were a boy it would probably be different. But you can see for yourself what's expected of a Catholic girl – marriage, and a brood of children . . . It's as if education doesn't matter for a girl. But I want to have more opportunities in my life. Anyway," she said quickly, "that wasn't what I wanted to ask you about."

"What was it, then?"

They had come to a standstill. Below them, the two arms of the harbour stretched out, and the figures of Cathal and Michael could be seen moving along the east pier. Beyond, the fitful sun made changing patterns on the surface of the sea: grey, aquamarine, a sudden sparkle and glint of reflected light.

"I asked you the other day do you disapprove of the Irish Volunteers," Siobhan said carefully.

"Yes. And I didn't answer because you got up and went home."

"You're an officer in the British Army. It'd be understandable if you did disapprove."

"Well," Patrick said slowly, "I don't. I'm an Irishman after all. And if circumstances had been different I might well have ended up in the Volunteers myself."

Siobhan nodded towards the figures of the two boys. "You know why they've gone down there?"

"To look at the boats, I suppose."

"They're looking at the place where the *Asgard* landed two years ago. You know, Erskine Childers' yacht, with the German rifles to arm the Volunteers. Donal was here that day. He helped unload the guns."

She was looking at him intently. Patrick knew that she was testing him, testing his loyalties. So Donal had helped with the gun-running, and was armed with a German rifle. He knew that the

142

more extreme members of the Irish Volunteers were trying to gain practical support wherever they could: from Clan na Gael in America, and from the Germans. He knew, too, that the Howth gun-running had been followed by the Bachelor's Walk incident, in which soldiers of the King's Own Scottish Borderers had opened fire on a jeering crowd, killing four civilians. The shooting had turned out to be a mistake, but the civilians were dead all the same. It was one of those incidents for which the British in Ireland seemed to have a special talent, he thought: the equivalent of throwing a lighted match into an ammunition dump.

"I suppose," he said, "for myself, I'd prefer it if Ireland stood alone in the fight for independence. We serve neither King nor Kaiser –"

"But Ireland," Siobhan finished. "But what use would the Volunteers or the Citizen Army be without weapons? The Ulster Volunteers are allowed to have them. And there are other deals with Germany going on even now."

It was true enough, Patrick thought. There were two voices in his head arguing with each other. The voice of the army officer said *It is treason – negotiating with Britain's enemy at a time of war.* The Irish voice argued back, *How can it be treason? Why should we be loyal to England's king and government? We didn't ask to be ruled by them. They are no more to us than the Kaiser, or the Tsar of Russia.* He did not know which voice spoke the louder. He had always wanted Ireland to be free, but was not sure whether he wanted it at any price. And having been away for so long he was out of touch with current affairs. He felt out of his depth, treading water.

"You've heard the rumours that there will be an armed uprising in Dublin?" Siobhan continued.

"Yes."

"What do you think about it?"

Patrick hesitated, not sure why he was being questioned so closely. Was Siobhan trying to recruit him for the Volunteers? Again, the two sides of his upbringing put him at odds with himself. His instinctive patriotism told him that an armed rising against the British forces would be completely justified. And yet, was it right to take advantage while English and Irish alike were fighting and dying in the trenches of Flanders?

"The English government has asked for it in a way," he said, trying to marshall his thoughts into some sort of order, "by threatening conscription. Why should Irish people, who've been persecuted by the English for hundreds of years, be made to fight for England? And for those who've volunteered already – it makes it meaningless. As Uncle James said, Brendan enlisted because it was his free choice. If there had been conscription then, he'd sooner have died first."

As he spoke, he remembered Cathal's suggestion that Brendan had had other reasons for enlisting, motives which now seemed highly plausible in view of his association with Donal. He realised that Siobhan must think him naive, to say what he had just said. But she nodded, and said, "Yes. And the rumours are true. There will be a rising."

"How can you be so sure?"

She hesitated, staring out beyond the harbour

144

wall to the faint misty outline of the Mountains of Mourne to the north. Loose strands of her hair, pulled free from their pinnings by the strong breeze, whipped back from her face. After a few moments she said, turning to face Patrick, "I want to tell you something concerning Cathal. But first you'll have to promise me that if I tell you what I know about the rising you won't say a word to anyone else. Anyone else at all."

"You mean the authorities at the Castle?"

Her eyes widened. "I didn't think you'd do that. Not after what you've said. I meant that I don't want to tell Mary – she's so . . ." She paused, biting her lip while she searched for the right word. "Innocent. It would upset her terribly. And I don't want to do the wrong thing for Cathal. So you're the best person to help."

Not at all sure what he was letting himself in for, Patrick said, "All right. I promise not to repeat whatever you tell me. But how can I help?"

"When it starts – and I don't know when that will be – Cathal will want to be in it. It's Donal's fault really – he's been encouraging Cathal, training him with a rifle, making him think he can be a hero for Ireland. I've tried to stop Donal from doing it, but I can't. Donal's old enough to decide for himself whether he wants to be a martyr, but Cathal's too young. Most of them know what the risks are, and most of them are going into it with full knowledge of that. They're prepared to be killed. And the only thing I can think of is for you to stop Cathal from going when the time comes."

They had begun to walk on again, slowly. Patrick

plucked a long stem of grass and twirled it in his fingers, thinking hard.

"But Cathal hates the sight of me. I should think if I tried to stop him, it would only make him all the more determined," he said. "Wouldn't it be better just to tell my aunt and uncle?"

"It's a question of timing. You don't know how desperate Cathal is. It means everything to him. If he thought beforehand that anyone would stop him from going with Donal, he'd run away from home."

"What about Michael? He's only the same age as Cathal. Aren't you just as worried about him?"

Siobhan shook her head. "No. He likes the . . . the whiff of danger, the defiance, but only at second-hand. And I have some influence over him, but none over Cathal. I've already made Michael promise me that he won't get involved. But Cathal's different."

What did she expect him to do, Patrick wondered? Kidnap Cathal, or knock him on the head, or imprison him in his room? But he knew that she was right. Cathal was too young to be allowed to sacrifice himself in some romantic notion of dying for his country. He could well believe that Cathal was determined enough to run away from home if he thought he would be thwarted. For all his cousin's adolescent gaucheness, there was an underlying sense of purpose and resolution. And, objectionable though Cathal had been, Patrick did not want to see him risk his life in some hopeless bid for glory.

"How do you know so much?" he asked. "About the uprising, about what Donal does, I mean?"

Siobhan gave a rueful half-smile. "He has people round to the house, for secret meetings in his room. I often – well, overhear things. And sometimes he tells me. He will tell me as soon as he knows when it's to be."

A thought struck Patrick. "I might not be in the country even, by that time. I'm due to go before a Medical Board in two weeks."

"It will be before then," Siobhan said.

Pearse

"It's obvious Siobhan's taken a liking to you," Mary said, a shade wistfully, as the family left the house for church on the morning of Palm Sunday.

"Oh, I don't think so. Not particularly." Patrick had seen the exchange of significant glances when he and Siobhan had returned from their walk at Howth, and had realised that both Mary and Bridget suspected romantic interest. "She wanted to ask me about applying for university," he said on impulse. The lie came easily, to his regret. He did not like lying to Mary.

However, she would not be shaken from her original idea. "Well, and I'm not surprised you enjoy talking to her. It must make a nice change for you to have interesting company."

"Oh, Mary, of course not," he protested against the slight she had implied against herself.

At the same time, it occurred to him that it might be useful to nurture the fiction of a romance. He would certainly need to see Siobhan again, preferably on her own, and soon – he already had dozens of questions he wanted to ask – and he could hardly tell Mary the real reason for seeking her out. He felt bad, after all the trouble Mary had taken with him, about neglecting her at the picnic, and he would need to do so again, unavoidably giving the impression that he preferred Siobhan's company to hers. He decided to make it up to her by presenting her with the finished portrait, which he had recently framed, with Uncle James' help. He was rather pleased with it. It was the best portrait he had ever drawn, and was mildly flattering to Mary while capturing her most characteristic expression of open-natured kindliness.

Sitting in church, he found himself quite unable to give his mind to the sermon. He wondered what Siobhan would be doing at this moment. Presumably, she would attend mass with her family, and would go to confession. What would she confess to? And her brother . . . *I am armed with a German Mauser, and I will kill people with it in the name of freedom* . . . What could a priest say to that?

He couldn't imagine, from what she had said, that she was strict in her religious practices; she was too independent to allow herself to be tied down. He knew little about Roman Catholicism; in his mind it was a huge, mysterious, flamboyant, shadowy, incense-smelling physical presence, to which the majority of the Irish nation belonged. But there were too many labels, he thought, Irish, English, German, Roman Catholic, Protestant: too many ways of dividing people who often had more in common than they had differences.

Later that afternoon, when Mary was alone in the garden, Patrick fetched the portrait from his room and brought it to her. She was sitting on the garden bench, sewing, beneath the lilac tree, and the powerful sweet scent of the heavy blooms reminded Patrick sharply of Edward carrying the limp body of Seamus back from Bell Common. A smear of blood on Edward's forearm . . . why had that detail remained in his mind with such clarity?

Mary took the framed drawing with an exclamation of surprise. "I didn't know you'd finished it! It's lovely, Patrick. I mean," she said in confusion, "you've made me look better than I look really, but it's a lovely picture. And you've got it framed. What will you do with it?"

He sat down beside her on the bench.

"I'm giving it to you."

"Oh, but –" She seemed disappointed. "Thank you, of course, thank you very much. But wouldn't you rather have it for yourself after all your work?"

"No – I did it for you. It's to thank you for looking after me."

"It's a pleasure, Patrick. You shouldn't be after thanking me. There's no need."

She moved closer to him and kissed him, and he saw that she looked almost tearful. He realised that she would have preferred it if he had wanted to keep the portrait himself, for sentimental reasons.

It seemed that he couldn't avoid hurting her feelings, no matter how hard he tried to avoid it.

He still hadn't solved the problem of how to meet Siobhan again. He could hardly go round to the MacBrides and ask her whether she knew any more about the uprising in full hearing of anyone who happened to be in the shop. And besides, she wouldn't be there so often now that she had started her training as an ambulance driver. Presumably she would get a message to him when she thought it necessary, but he was reluctant just to sit and wait when there was so much more he wanted to know.

Since the conversation at Howth, he had observed Cathal carefully and had decided that Siobhan was probably right in what she had said. Cathal, as usual, had little to say in Patrick's presence, but there was a sense of edginess and concealed excitement about him. He was on holiday from school now for Easter, and was frequently out of the house, returning for meals and to sleep, spending much of his time at the MacBrides' or elsewhere.

On Tuesday morning, Patrick decided that he would write Siobhan a note. She must have some time off work, or perhaps he could meet her in the city and walk back with her; that would give them plenty of time for a private conversation. He wrote a short note, sealed it in an envelope and went round to the shop, where he asked Mrs MacBride to give it to Siobhan that evening.

Mrs MacBride leaned across the counter and took the envelope in extended fingers as if it were something she would prefer not to touch.

"I'll see she gets it," she said.

Patrick noted her faint sniff of disapproval. Obviously she thought it was a billet-doux; as a strict Catholic she would not want to encourage her daughter's friendship with a young man nominally of the Protestant faith. Patrick hoped that she would pass on the note nevertheless. Her suspicion of romance would be short-lived, at any rate: his remaining time in Dublin had shrunk to a matter of days.

The next morning, Roisin brought round a note from Siobhan in return, saying that she would meet him outside in Bewley's cafe in Westmoreland Street at three o'clock that afternoon. Patrick's next practical problem was how to divert Mary; if he said that he was going into the city she would almost certainly offer to come with him. Finally, he realised that if he told the truth, that he was meeting Siobhan, Mary would put her own interpretation on it and would stay at home. He didn't like misleading her, but could see no alternative.

It was a day of sunshine interspersed with showers, like so many recent days. He left home early in order to go the art suppliers' for more drawing-paper, and then having time on his hands walked round by the Castle before going on to Westmoreland Street. A convoy of ambulances, some of them converted vehicles of the Royal Irish Automobile Club, entered the courtyard as he passed, carrying wounded soldiers from the station or the harbour: a large part of the Castle had been handed over for use as a Red Cross hospital. Above the armed soldier at the gate was the bronze figure of justice, scales in hand, "its face to the Castle, its back to the nation," as the cynical Dublin saying had it. Inside the gates, Patrick glimpsed the ambulances passing the Chapel Royal and on through the archway leading to the splendid State apartments. It was an incongruous hospital, although, he supposed, no more incongruous than a luxury cruiser.

It occurred to him that the Castle, with its symbolic and actual significance as the seat of British rule, would surely be one of the targets for the rebel troops in what could be only a matter of days. Men could be fighting and dying where he stood. The idea sent a tremor through him of excitement tinged with fear. Surely the authorities would get wind of the rising, and disarm the Volunteers? Or were they so confident that the rebellion would easily be put down, and posed no real threat? He thought of Siobhan's situation, working under the eye of the authorities while knowing full well what was likely to occur. It took nerve and coolness, he thought, both of which she seemed to possess in good measure. Her position was even more ambivalent than his own: she seemed to be in favour of the Rising in principle although sure that it would be suppressed; she was supporting the war effort through her Red Cross work, yet had the partial confidence of a brother who was plotting the overthrow of British rule.

How many similar families were there in Ireland, he thought, pulled in all directions at once?

He walked along Dame Street and College Green to the new Bewley's cafe in a sudden fall of soft rain. There was no sign of Siobhan outside, just a young woman in navy-blue who was looking in the direction of O'Connell Bridge. While he stood waiting, a girl of about his own age, dressed shabbily in a dusty serge skirt which dragged along the pavement, came along the street asking passers-by for money; she held a baby in one arm while another infant trailed along clinging to the edge of her shawl. Struck by the thinness and pallor of the girl's face and the hopeless wailing of the child, Patrick found a sixpence in his pocket and dropped it in the outstretched palm.

"God love you, sorr." The girl was pathetically grateful, bobbing a curtsey and thanking him out of all proportion to the sum he had given her. Beggars were a common enough sight in the streets of

Dublin, but Patrick felt disturbed by the encounter. Why should a young woman of twenty or so be reduced to begging on the streets to provide for her children and herself?

"Patrick." He felt a touch on his arm, and turned to see the young lady in blue standing behind him. It was Siobhan, dressed in uniform, with a collar and tie and a soft brimmed hat.

"Siobhan, I'm sorry. I didn't recognise you in that uniform."

She looked down at the long ill-fitting skirt and shapeless jacket, and then smiled at him. "It isn't flattering exactly, is it?"

"Well . . ." He looked her up and down and then said honestly, "Not altogether."

"But, well – " She nodded in the direction of the girl who had just passed them. "I shouldn't complain about it. Shall we go inside out of the rain?"

"If you'd like to. Have you finished for the day?"

"I've two hours off. Then I'm back on duty till ten o'clock. Elementary first aid this week, and doing the rounds with an experienced driver. Then it'll be mechanical training. And then I'll be doing a proper job at last."

They went inside and sat down at a table with large wooden pews as seats. A waitress came and took their order for tea, and Patrick looked around the crowded cafe, doubtful about whether they could talk any more freely here than in the MacBrides' shop. Siobhan, understanding, said, "We'll go outside for a walk afterwards. If you've time."

"Of course I have."

With the real object of their meeting thus deferred,

Patrick wondered what to talk about instead. The waitress brought the tea, and Siobhan poured it out, and then said, "It can't be very pleasant for you, the idea of going back to your regiment."

"It seems a long way off still, although it's only a week. I've tried not to think about it much. And there's been a lot to distract my attention here in Dublin."

As he spoke, it struck him that some girls would have interpreted the remark as a personal compliment. Siobhan obviously didn't. She nodded, and said quietly, "Yes. It seems hard to think that life will go on after Sunday."

He looked at her. "You mean that's when –"

"Yes. But I'll tell you more later on."

It would be happening, then, and soon. In four days' time. Sunday would be April 23rd, St. George's Day. Perhaps the date had been deliberately chosen for that reason, the ideal day to strike a blow against English complacency.

"On Monday, Bank Holiday," he said, "We're all supposed to be going to the races at Fairyhouse, to see the Grand National. Someone whose portrait Uncle James is commissioned to paint has invited him and the whole family for the day."

"That'll be grand."

They were both silent for a few moments, and Patrick knew that they were both thinking of how everything might have changed by Monday. The Fairyhouse races would probably be irrelevant by then, a pointless sideshow to the real drama taking place in the centre of the city.

"I haven't spoken to Cathal much since Saturday," he said. "He avoids me as much as he can, and I think he must go round to your house. But you might easily be right, what you said. I'm still not sure what to do about it though."

"Leave it until Sunday and then don't let him out of your sight."

Easier said than done, Patrick thought. Church would occupy a good deal of the morning; Cathal always went to church, so that would be simple enough. But then what? It still seemed to him that the safest thing would be to tell his aunt and uncle. If he didn't tell them until church on Sunday, Cathal wouldn't have time to do anything drastic.

He changed the subject. "What made you decide to enlist as an ambulance driver, and volunteer for overseas service? Do you see it as your duty?"

"In a way, yes. While Irish troops are fighting in Belgium and France it seems wrong just to let them get on with it when there's something practical to be done. I suppose what it means is that I support the Irish without supporting the war, if that's possible. I don't believe all that stuff about the heart of the earth being warmed by the red wine of battle, or any other heroic nonsense."

The phrase struck a chord. "That sounds like a quotation from Rupert Brooke."

"No, it's Patrick Pearse."

"Did he say that?"

"He wrote it."

Patrick frowned. The words were all too familiar, the words of someone who had not seen battle; stirring, but ultimately false. No-one who had seen even as little of real warfare as Patrick had would be able to write glibly about bloodshed as spilled red wine. And yet Pearse, ardent nationalist, poet, playwright and schoolteacher, a man of apparently inexhaustible energies, was someone he had always greatly admired.

"I heard him at Jeremiah O'Donovan Rossa's funeral last August," Siobhan said, as if following the same train of thought. "Did you read about it in the papers? He's a wonderful speaker. He had the whole crowd there ready to die for him. Even people who knew nothing about O'Donovan Rossa. *Ireland unfree shall never be at peace* . . . If you'd been there and heard him say those things, you'd have wanted to die for him. No, die for Ireland. He's a wonderful speaker because he believes entirely in what he says, so strongly that he carries other people along with him."

"Yes. I can see that."

"Either he's a truly great man," Siobhan said slowly, "or he's insane. Or perhaps both at once."

Two army officers were making their way between the rows of tables. They sat down at the adjoining bench, spreading their booted legs out into the aisle and placing their caps on the table. Further conversation was impossible.

"So have you any other errands to do in town?" Siobhan said, looking at the brown paper parcel with the new sketchpad in it.

"Uncle James asked me to get him some pipe tobacco." Patrick looked at his watch. "Come on, let's go outside."

They finished their tea quickly and went out into the warm, damp afternoon. Westmoreland Street was crowded with people going to and from the commercial streets of the centre; it had stopped raining. On Patrick's suggestion that there would be fewer people about by the riverside, they set off in that direction, waiting to cross the busy junction by O'Connell Bridge. When Mary walked out with him, she usually hurried along beside him with quick tripping steps and often took hold of his arm; it occurred to him now that it would be rather nice if Siobhan did the same, and that it would be perfectly in order for him to take her arm while they were crossing the road. However, when the junction was clear Siobhan strode across so fast that he had to dodge quickly between a cab and a coster's barrow to keep up with her.

They stopped at Burgh Quay, where they leaned on the parapet and looked across at Liberty Hall.

"That's been there since the beginning of Holy Week," Siobhan said, pointing to the green flag with an uncrowned harp which fluttered from the flagstaff on its roof as if challenging the Union Jack outside the Custom House.

"Is that wise? It looks like a declaration."

"The Citizen Army on its own is too small to worry the government, I suppose."

"The Volunteers and the Citizen Army will join forces?" Patrick couldn't help dropping his voice to a whisper, even though there was no-one within earshot.

"Yes. It will be on Sunday evening. It's been generally publicised that there will be manoeuvres – you know, the normal sort of thing, parading about, so it doesn't look like anything out of the ordinary. It's really a cover for the Rising. They're going to attack the General Post Office over there as the main headquarters, with other outposts all round the city, and declare a Republic, with Pearse as the President."

"Pearse is one of the leaders?"

"Yes, with Connolly and MacDonagh and others, but there have been all sorts of rows going on about it. It seems that most of the Volunteers don't know a thing about what's really happening on Sunday, not even Eoin MacNeill, who's supposed to be their Chief of Staff. He'd never support it. A small group of the IRB have arranged it all behind his back. Pearse among them."

"How do you know so much about it? Did Donal tell you all this?"

"No. But he had some IRB people round to talk in his room, and I listened through the wall with a glass. I needed to know," Siobhan said matter-of-factly.

Patrick looked at her. Her neat features were turned in profile as she gazed across the river in the direction of Nelson's pillar in Sackville Street. He thought she was quite a remarkable girl, and wondered what her reaction would be if he were to tell her so. Probably she would think him patronising; she did not seek or expect compliments or gallant behaviour.

"It's going to rain again," he said, looking up at the darkening sky. "Come on. I'll walk with you back to the Castle."

"If you've time. You could just as easily get your tram back from College Green."

"No, I'd like to."

"Well, if you're sure."

They walked back the way they had come, waiting

again at the O'Connell Bridge junction. This time Patrick felt emboldened to take her arm before she dashed across. She did not resist, but detached herself as soon as they reached the safety of Aston Quay, rather to his disappointment.

Weeding

Good Friday morning brought Patrick a letter from Edward.

"Things are rather quiet out here at present," Edward wrote, *"in so far as life in the front line ever can be quiet. Two men in my platoon were killed yesterday by a casual shell which came over while they were cooking their breakfast bacon; regrettably, one soon learns to accept incidents like that as commonplace. We are due to come out of the line in two days' time, so I am looking forward to a comfortable billet in a French farmhouse well out of Fritz's artillery range. More likely it will turn out to be a tent or a leaky barn instead.*

The French seem to be bearing the brunt at the moment, and if it goes on for much longer it seems probable that there will be a new push on our part to take the pressure off them.

I am both pleased and concerned to know that you are fully recovered and will be rejoining us, subject to Medical Board. I thought when you left hospital that you had bought your Blighty ticket for once and for all. Now, I suppose, you will be widening your travel experience to include the doubtful delights of the Western Front. On the positive side, perhaps we will meet again sooner than expected. I have some interesting news which I will keep until then. Give my best regards to your aunt, uncle and cousins. Is it true that there is going to be trouble in Ireland? If so, keep your head down . . ."

Patrick read the letter twice, wondering what Edward could have meant by "interesting news". Had Edward been promoted again? He had quickly been awarded the second pip of full lieutenant; perhaps by now he had progressed to Captain. Patrick remembered that he had had a prominent role in Officer Training Corps during their schooldays. It was odd that Edward, the gentlest and least aggressive of people, should prove to be so successful as a soldier. He hated any kind of cruelty, and had never shown any interest at all in shooting or fox-hunting, the traditional country pastimes of his class. By now Edward would have been thoroughly tested under fire, and had presumably shown the required steadiness. Patrick, with the prospect of his return to the army looming ever closer, was acutely conscious that he himself was untried, apart from his one brief and disastrous excursion into enemy fire. How would he cope with trench warfare?

He was uneasily aware that he would soon find out.

And, remembering his friend's obvious distress when they had met soon after the fighting at Loos, he realised that Edward's military achievements did not come easily to him. He wasn't the dashing sort of officer who saw war as a great lark. The brisk, even jaunty style of the letter seemed to reveal a different Edward, the side of him, perhaps, which he presented to his army superiors. To lead his platoon effectively into combat, he must have had to overcome his natural revulsion for killing. Patrick remembered bayonet drill, when they had had to stab and impale sacks on the ground. Had Edward ever had to do that to a human being?

"Is that from your father?" Mary asked, coming into the room as Patrick folded the letter back into its envelope.

"No, from Edward. From France."

Mary sighed. "The poor dear. I wish this terrible war would finish quickly. What does he say?"

"Not much. It seems to be just routine. But he wouldn't be allowed to give details in any case."

"Send him our love when you write back," Mary said. "It seems a long time since we saw him. He was such a lovely young man."

Patrick wished she wouldn't speak of Edward in the past tense. The problem with receiving letters from the front was that the person writing had had time to be killed twenty times over by the time the letter was received. What would Edward say if he were here now, and they could sit down and have a good long chat about the situation in Ireland? Edward had just seen two of his men killed by a German shell; what would he think of Irish rebels armed with German rifles? And yet he had always been in favour of Irish independence, disdainful of imperialist pride and governmental foot-dragging. He had once told Patrick that Irish history made him feel ashamed to be English . . .

"Come and help me in the garden if you feel like some fresh air," Mary said. "If I don't get that long border tidy now it'll be a jungle by summer."

Stooping among the newly-emerging herbaceous plants with a trowel and trug, obediently yanking out weeds at Mary's direction, Patrick looked up at the back view of the house, remembering that he had intended to do a drawing for his aunt before he left. He must start this afternoon, he decided, or he wouldn't stand a chance of finishing before next Wednesday . . .

"This clematis did well last year," Mary said, "but I'll have to watch it doesn't strangle the laburnum. And look, the slugs have eaten nearly all those seedlings I put in."

. . . By Wednesday the Rising would be three days old . . . Would it be over by then, suppressed as briskly as Robert Emmet's two-hour rebellion? Or would Ireland be a Republic, triumphantly claiming her right to freedom? Either way, the events of Sunday were creeping inexorably closer, and here he was in a suburban garden thinking about drawings and slugs and seedlings . . . He looked where Mary pointed, and saw that the seedlings which had uncurled so confidently above the raked earth had been munched and nibbled, some of them showing only bare stalks, completely defeated.

"There's such a lot to do out here now that Mr Rourke's back's too bad for him to come any more," Mary continued. "Cathal said he'd help, but I've hardly seen the sight of him."

"Do you know where he is now?"

"Round at the MacBrides', I suppose. We've so many daffodils, I think I'll cut some for indoors – don't they look cheerful? He and Michael are as thick as thieves these days."

"Do you see much of the other brother, Donal?" Patrick turned his back towards Mary and carried on weeding assiduously. He was sure she would notice his falsely casual expression.

"No, not much. He's so tied up with the Volunteers. Always out on manoeuvres and parades and the like, and at meetings in town. It's such a pity that even respectable people like Patrick Pearse are at the forefront of it."

"Oh, yes?"

Mary straightened up with her bunch of daffodils. "It's a bit of a problem about Mr Pearse. St. Enda's used to be such a good school, but people aren't after sending their boys there the way they used to before Mr Pearse got so involved in all this rabble-rousing. It'll come to no good, I'm sure of it. I'll just take these indoors and put them in water before they droop, then we'll soon make headway with that border."

Left alone with the weeds, Patrick thought about Edward and Patrick Pearse. If Edward was a peace-loving soul who had had to steel himself to violence, Pearse seemed to be a character of far more extreme contradictions. According to Siobhan, he wouldn't allow a fly to be squashed unnecessarily, yet was quite prepared to squander his own life and those of his followers in what he saw as a blood sacrifice, out of which the new Ireland would grow.

"It's as if he wants to be make himself a martyr," she had said, "as if getting himself killed fighting British rule is all he's ever lived for."

Yet she had called him a great man. Patrick had seen Pearse only once at one of the school plays, a tall dark-haired man with a high forehead, a slight squint in one eye and a solemn, serene expression. He had been aware then of Pearse's charisma, a power stemming from his quiet strength and determination and his absolute pure faith in his principles. He could well believe that Pearse's followers were willing to do anything he asked.

And Pearse was Cathal's headmaster. With Pearse supplying the ideals and Donal MacBride the tactics of basic soldiering, it was hardly to be wondered at if Cathal refused to stay at home on Sunday.

Having imagined all sorts of fantastic and highly impractical solutions to the problem, Patrick had decided that the best plan was still the most obvious one: to wait until Sunday morning, then tell his aunt and uncle that there was to be a Rising and that he thought Cathal would join the rebels. Cathal would hate him for it, but that wasn't likely to make much difference. And if Cathal wanted to be a martyr for Ireland, there would doubtless be other chances for him in the future . . .

He heard the back door close and then footsteps on the gravel path. "Oh, you are doing well," Mary remarked, pleased.

He sat back on his heels to look at the result of his efforts, the unimpeded new growth in the border and the wooden trug piled with weeds and clods. The mental activity had made him work at ferocious speed. The soil, damp from the recent showers, smelled coolly fertile, crumbling to the touch. He supposed that it was British soil; every sod and stone in this garden belonged to Britain. Perhaps by Sunday evening it would be Irish soil . . . but no, he was letting himself drift into fantasy, enticed by the daring of the enterprise. Could a few hundred assorted Volunteers, armed with whatever weapons they could get their hands on, take on the might of the British Empire and hope to win? It would be like David confronting Goliath. But then, with one well-placed stone . . . Siobhan said that Pearse was confident in the support of people all over Ireland for the insurrection once they saw that it could succeed, and that Irish troops called in to restore order would refuse to fire on their fellow countrymen . . .

"I suppose you'll be seeing Siobhan again before you go back?" Mary asked.

Patrick recognised the note of deliberate nonchalance in her voice.

"I've no plans to," he said, with perfect truth. "She's busy with her work."

"Oh, she'll try to find the time surely? The two of you seemed to get on so well."

Patrick shrugged. "I don't know."

Mary glanced at him and then, as if suspecting that she had touched a sensitive spot, carried on jabbing at an obstinate thistle without saying any more.

Patrick had had it in mind since Wednesday that he did want to see Siobhan again, but was not sure how it could be arranged. He was beginning to wish that Mary's and Mrs MacBride's suspicions had some small basis in fact; Siobhan herself gave the impression that as long as he did what she asked regarding Cathal, she would be satisfied. It was quite possible that he would leave on the mail boat next week without setting eyes on her again.

Everything depended on what happened on Sunday.

He was beginning to feel anxious on her behalf. Supposing she happened to be at the Castle when fighting broke out? In their conversations, she had shown more concern for Cathal's safety than for her own. Had it so much as occurred to her that she too might be in danger?

Mary said, doubtfully, "Are you feeling all right, Patrick? You're very quiet today. Are you sure you're really fit enough to go back to the army so soon?"

"Oh – sorry." He would have to make a better effort. "No, I'm perfectly all right. Just thinking about the new picture I'm going to start. It should be a good day on Monday, shouldn't it? Have you ever been to the Grand National before?"

Easter Sunday

Late on Saturday afternoon, Patrick walked through the rain to the MacBrides' shop on the pretext of buying razor blades.

Mrs MacBride, measuring out tea at the counter, said sharply, "If it's Siobhan you're after seeing, she's not here."

"No, just the razor blades, thank you." Patrick handed over his money and pocketed the change and then said casually, "Is Cathal here?"

"He is not. He and Michael have gone into town with Donal, two hours since."

Patrick cursed himself silently. Why had he been so dense as to leave it so late? Cathal had gone, and might take the opportunity not to come home again, even though the Volunteer manoeuvres were not due to begin for more than twenty-four hours; he might want to make absolutely sure of his freedom while he had the chance. What should he do now?

"Do you know where they went?" he asked Mrs MacBride.

She looked at him from under lowered brows and carried on spooning tea into the scales, so that the air in the shop seemed full of its dry perfumey scent. "I've no idea."

Patrick wondered how much she did know. If Donal was a member of the secretive Irish Republican Brotherhood and held meetings in his bedroom, she must have a shrewd enough idea of his activities. But she obviously wasn't going to give Patrick any help.

"Are you expecting them back?" he persisted.

She gave him another odd look. "Don't they live here?"

He decided to go back home, wait for another hour and then, if Cathal still hadn't appeared, go into town to look for him. If Donal had gone too, he thought it possible that all three had gone to the Liberty Hall Headquarters. If not, he would have no idea at all where to look next. Why hadn't he told his aunt sooner of what he suspected? They could have locked Cathal in his room if necessary. It wouldn't have been Patrick's problem any more. But, he reasoned, Cathal would simply deny it, and his aunt and uncle, never prone to unnecessary fuss, would have thought Patrick was making a melodrama out of nothing, leaving Cathal free to slip away during the night or early next morning. Well, if he did return, Patrick was determined not to let him out of his sight.

The hour he had set himself dragged past. Unable to turn his mind to anything else, Patrick waited in the drawing-room, which had a view of the road outside. Soon Mary came in and found him there, and brought in tea, and he had to force himself to sit calmly and make conversation. It was raining harder; a horse clopped by outside, car tyres swished on the wet road, pedestrians hurried past the window, huddled beneath umbrellas. At last, he could bear the inactivity no longer. Without saying anything to Mary, he went out into the hall and took his coat from the hatstand peg.

As he did so, he saw the shadowy outline of a figure behind the stained-glass of the front door, and then a key turned in the latch and Cathal came in.

They stared at each other. Cathal's wet hair stuck to his forehead, drops of water trickled slowly down his face and the shoulders of his jacket showed dark with rain. His lower lip trembled and for a moment Patrick thought he was going to burst into tears. He looked utterly stricken, his face gaunt and his eyes blank with incomprehension.

"Cathal, whatever's the matter?" Patrick moved instinctively towards him.

Cathal simply gazed back as if he had never seen him before.

Patrick heard an exclamation behind him and Mary came into the hallway, pushing past him to seize her brother by the arm. "Cathal, you're *soaked*. Whatever were you thinking of to get yourself so drenched? Why didn't you shelter somewhere until the rain stopped? Go and change out of those wet things and bring them down to me. I'll make you some hot tea, and you can sit by the fire and warm up."

She chivvied him up the stairs. He climbed slowly, his head bent, looking like a tired old man. Patrick and Mary exchanged concerned glances.

"He'll be lucky if he doesn't catch a cold, the idiot boy," Mary said. She went into the kitchen to put the kettle on, and Patrick was left standing in the hallway wondering what on earth could have happened. He would have expected Cathal to be keyed-up with secret excitement, the very opposite of the abject despair written on his face. Had Donal forbidden him to join the Volunteers on Sunday after all? But would Cathal be likely to obey such an instruction, even from someone he looked up to?

Baffled, Patrick went into the kitchen to help Mary. Ten minutes later, when Cathal had not reappeared, he said, "I'll take his cup of tea up to him in his room."

"Well, all right," Mary said doubtfully.

He went upstairs, knocked on Cathal's door and went in. Cathal was lying face down on his bed, his arm dangling loosely to the floor. He looked up briefly and then let his head flop down again, not even protesting as Patrick entered the room. He had not changed out of his wet clothes, and Patrick saw that he was crying. His first thought was that something terrible must have happened. An accident? A shooting? Some-one killed? He sat down on the edge of the bed.

"Cathal, please tell me what's wrong," he said. "Are you ill, or hurt? Would you like me to fetch Mary or your mother?"

Cathal's eyes were closed, tears squeezing between the dark lashes. He choked back a sob in his throat. Patrick, oddly touched, felt helpless in the face of such distress. Rather awkwardly, he put his hand on his cousin's shoulder. He expected Cathal to shake it off or to react angrily, but instead he continued to sob, taking no notice of the gesture. Then he rolled over and sniffed, and Patrick found his own clean handkerchief in his pocket and handed it to him. Their hands touched briefly as Cathal fumbled for it.

"You're cold!" Patrick exclaimed. "Look, you must change out of these damp things. Will I fetch someone?" he said again, concerned more than anything by Cathal's unusual passivity. This, more than anything, convinced him that he had had some dreadful experience.

Cathal propped himself up to blow his nose and then lay down again, turning his face to the wall.

"No," he said dully, "don't fetch anyone. I'll be all right. You can leave me alone now."

"Only if you stop crying, and change your clothes, and tell me what's the matter."

He got up from the bed and started looking in Cathal's wardrobe for suitable garments. Cathal sat upright, still sniffing, and looked at him with something like his usual expression.

"I can't tell you. It isn't anything you'd understand."

"It might be," Patrick said cautiously.

Cathal shook his head, but stood up slowly and started to unbutton his trousers. His tears were under control now. Patrick, respecting his privacy, said, "Well, I'll leave you to get dressed. But promise me you'll come downstairs. Mary's worried about you."

Patrick woke early on Easter Sunday morning to see the light filtering palely through his bedroom curtains. He got out of bed and went across the landing to the lavatory, then crept to Cathal's door and listened intently. He could just hear the boy's regular breathing. Reassured that Cathal hadn't disappeared during the night, he went back to his own room, and sat on the edge of the bed, thinking.

Neither Mary nor Aunt Margaret had been able to find out from Cathal what had upset him so deeply. Patrick, sure that it was something to do with the Rising, was relieved nevertheless. After his anxiety of earlier in the day when he thought he had let his cousin slip, he knew that Cathal was at least in the house. Cathal had come downstairs for the evening meal, quiet and subdued, had eaten little, and had gone to bed early. Mary had been convinced that he was going down with some illness, and had fetched him hot lemon drinks, extra blankets and a hot water bottle, all of which he had refused. It had occurred to Patrick at one stage that the whole thing could be an act, leading up to a midnight disappearance. But he rejected the idea as soon as he thought of it. Cathal's wretchedness was clearly genuine, and his behaviour was not that of someone planning the greatest adventure of his life for the following day.

Now, sitting on his bed and noticing abstractedly that his toenails needed cutting, Patrick thought of the day ahead. He would get washed and dressed, have breakfast and go to church, while all around the city guns and ammunition were hidden in cellars and sheds, ready; those in the know would be getting up, going to mass, taking communion, confessing, aware that this could be the last Sunday of their lives. He was aware of a thrill of excitement, coupled with a sense of regret that he would have only a bystander's role. The domestic details which would occupy the day seemed enormously irrelevant to the real stuff of life in Dublin today, history in the making.

He remembered that he had thought exactly the same thing before the Gallipoli landings. It was not a good omen.

Cathal did not come downstairs for breakfast, and as Patrick came out of his room he overheard voices raised in argument, Cathal's and Aunt Margaret's.

"I keep telling you I'm not ill. I don't want medicine."

"Well, in that case you can get dressed and come to church with us."

Patrick left them to it, and went down to the dining-room. Uncle James, who had already finished breakfast, was sitting at the table reading the Sunday Independent. Mary came in with the coffee-pot, wearing her best frill-necked blouse and cameo brooch ready for church, with a flowered apron for protection while she did her kitchen chores. They wished each other a happy Easter, and then Uncle James put down the folded newspaper and said, "Well, I must do some work before church. Excuse me."

Patrick poured coffee for himself and Mary. Glancing at the newpaper, he saw that there was a notice in bold type on the page facing him. The words *Irish Volunteers* leapt out of the page. He leaned over and read:

Owing to the very critical position, all orders given to the Irish Volunteers for tomorrow, Easter Sunday, are hereby rescinded, and no parades, marches, or other movements of the Irish Volunteers will take place. Each individual Volunteer will obey this order strictly in every particular.

Patrick stared at it, comprehension dawning. The marches and manoeuvres scheduled for this evening had been a cover for the Rising. The newspaper announcement would be understood by everyone who had known of the real plans: the Rising was cancelled.

His mind was a turmoil. He understood now why Cathal had come home in such a state; he had probably been to Liberty Hall, and had heard of the cancellation yesterday. But what had gone wrong? Had the Castle authorities got wind of what was in the air? Had the leaders been arrested? It must be something as drastic as that for the leaders to throw away what must have been months of work, plans, preparations. The Rising was cancelled. Cathal was safe. Patrick felt almost dizzy with a rush of confused emotions. He read the notice a second time to make sure he had understood correctly. No, there could be no mistaking its meaning . . .

Aunt Margaret came into the room. "Good morning, Patrick. A happy Easter to you."

"And the same to yourself, aunt." He turned the newspaper over, not wanting the announcement to be the subject of breakfast discussion. Why did he see himself in a protective role, he wondered, shielding Cathal, shielding everyone else in the family from finding out what had so nearly come about? And did it matter any more?

He couldn't face breakfast. He finished his coffee and stood up. Mary, glancing at his unused plate, said, "Are you not eating anything, Patrick?"

"Sorry, I'm not hungry this morning."

As he left the room, he heard Mary saying to her mother, "I'm sure he and Cathal are going down with 'flu."

"You worry too much," Aunt Margaret replied. "They're big healthy lads, the pair of them."

Patrick went up to his room to get ready for church. He could hardly believe that it was going to be a perfectly ordinary Sunday. Nothing to go down in the history books after all. It would be a rebellion that never happened. He felt stunned, as if he had suddenly heard that the war was over – but no, it was more complex than that. His relief was mixed with other feelings. Cathal was safe, but so was British rule. Ireland would stay British. Nelson's statue would continue to look down smugly at the Dublin people from its column in Sackville Street, an unchallenged imperial presence. The war against Germany would go on, and Irish soldiers would continue to go willingly to the meaningless slaughter, for England.

Although he had not been at all sure whether or not he supported the Rising, he now, perversely, found himself thrown into a mood of despondency by its cancellation. Wearily, he straightened his tie in front of the mirror and put on his jacket. He thought of Brendan standing here in front of the glass. What would Brendan have been thinking now, if he had lived? Probably, he would have thought that any patriotic Irishman should lie down and die of shame.

Now, there was nothing ahead but the Fairyhouse Races tomorrow and then the mail-boat on Wednesday.

The day passed slowly and uneventfully by. Cathal, still subdued, gave in to his mother and went with the rest of the family to the Easter service. After lunch, Patrick sat on the garden bench working half-heartedly at his drawing of the house; Uncle James painted in his studio; Mary sewed; Aunt Margaret did the household accounts.

Cathal spent most of the day in his room. At tea-time Mary, looking anxious, came into the garden to find Patrick.

"Cathal says he isn't well," she said. "I knew he wasn't himself."

Patrick's pencil hovered to a standstill over a difficult piece of shading around the roof gables.

"What's the matter with him?"

"I don't know. Mother's with him now, taking his temperature. I said we shouldn't have made him get up and go to church. I think he's getting the 'flu. He hardly ate anything at lunch and now he doesn't want any tea."

A few moments later Aunt Margaret came out of the house, shaking the thermometer, and said, "He's got a slight temperature. You were right, Mary. It's so disappointing, with the races tomorrow. Cathal obviously won't be able to go."

"I'll stay at home with him," Mary offered promptly.

"But there's no reason for you to miss the races," her mother said. "You deserve an outing. You can go with your father and Patrick, and I'll stay."

Patrick thought quickly. There was no longer any need for him to feel responsible for Cathal, but for some reason he still did. And he did not want Mary or his aunt to miss the Bank Holiday outing they had been looking forward to.

"No," he said. "You two go to the races. I don't mind staying here."

Aunt Margaret looked from Patrick to her daughter and back again with an expression of wry amusement. "Well, it sounds as if none of us wants to go. Perhaps we should simply call the whole thing off."

"But Mr Fitzgibbon will have made arrangements," Mary objected. "And it's an important commission for Father. He won't want to risk losing it. It'd be silly for us all not to go."

Aunt Margaret hesitated, and Patrick said, "It's obvious you should both go. I really don't mind staying behind. I don't much like horse-racing anyway."

"Oh Patrick, you *do*." Mary looked at him, and her eyes widened in concern. "Are you getting the 'flu as well? I've thought for a few days you haven't seemed yourself altogether."

Patrick remembered the snatch of conversation he had overheard earlier. Taking advantage, he said, "Well, I do feel a little off colour. I'd be quite happy to stay at home and look after Cathal and finish this." He indicated the sketch-pad which rested on his knees. It was the second time he had lied to Mary, but he thought it justified by his wish that she should have an enjoyable day out.

"Oh, but if you're not well either then I'll stay at home and look after the pair of you," Mary said at once.

"No, no, I don't need looking after," he said hastily. "And I do want you to go. I don't want to spoil your Bank Holiday for you."

"It won't be the same at the races if you don't come," Mary said regretfully.

"Of course it will. You'll have a grand day out."

At last both Mary and Aunt Margaret agreed to Patrick's suggestion, but Mary was convinced that he was concealing serious illness from her, and he spent the rest of the evening refusing offers of hot toddies, cough linctus and bedsocks.

The Wearing of the Green

After the days of changeable, showery weather, Easter Monday was warm and sunny. Mary and her parents appeared in their smartest clothes to wait for the motor-car which was to take them to Fairyhouse. Mary, rather self-consciously wearing a broad-brimmed hat with white pleating underneath, deluged Patrick with last-minute instructions.

"There's a cold pie in the larder . . . and you will remember to give Cathal plenty of drinks, won't you? . . . I've written the doctor's address on a notepad on the dining table . . ."

"Come on, Mary. The car's here," her father called from the front window.

Mary dithered in the kitchen, overcome by last-minute doubts. "It seems awful to leave you here, Patrick. Are you sure you wouldn't go instead of me?"

"Yes, I am sure. And you're all dressed and lovely in your finery. Now off you go and enjoy yourself."

He pushed her through the doorway before she could think of anything else to tell him. Giving in, she went out of the house and got into the back seat of the car beside her mother. Patrick stood on the front doorstep and waved as the vehicle pulled away, with Mary clutching at her hat.

He went back indoors, where the heavy silence of the house settled around him like a cloak. The fine weather would give him a good opportunity to finish the drawing; he wanted to get it framed by tomorrow evening. He had just two days left. He wondered whether he would be able to see Siobhan again; perhaps, as soon as the family returned, he'd go round to the shop and leave a note for her. He wanted to see her, briefly at least, to know what she thought of the cancellation of the Rising. And for other reasons besides. He wanted to ask if he could write to her after he had gone, and whether she would write back.

Assembling his pencils, eraser and sketch-book, Patrick thought of his reasons for declining to go to the races. It was true that he wanted to finish his picture, but there was another motive besides. He had a vague idea of having a conversation with Cathal. Now that the tensions of the supposed Rising were over, he thought there was some chance of success; it would be better for everyone if the relationship between himself and his cousin were on an amicable footing before he left. He would want to come back to Dublin, after all, and Aunt Margaret had told him that he could come whenever his leave arrangements permitted. And on Saturday, Cathal had been – well, not friendly, but not hostile either. It was worth a try.

He opened his sketch-pad, where the half-finished drawing was protected from smudging by a layer of tissue. There was still a lot to do, in particular the details of the trees and shrubs, which he found difficult. Caricatures he could draw in minutes flat, but with what he thought of as a proper drawing he was painstakingly slow and careful. He frowned at the sketch, wondering if he had got the perspecive quite right . . .

There was a knocking at the front door. He went to answer it and found Roisin MacBride standing there. She was wearing a summery straw boater, and beneath its brim her dark eyes regarded him with the cool stare he had found so disconcerting before.

"Is Cathal here?" she asked, without any preliminary greeting.

"He is, but he's upstairs in his room. He's ill with the 'flu."

Roisin held out an envelope. "I've brought a message for him. It's from Michael. Can you see he gets it?"

"Yes, of course."

He took the note from her. She looked at him, unsmiling, and then turned abruptly, the ribbons of her hat flying out and then settling over the dark glossy fall of her hair. Patrick closed the door and walked slowly up the stairs, turning the sealed envelope slowly in his hands. He wondered what it was about the girl's inscrutable stare that he found so unsettling. *An Roisin Dubh*, he found himself thinking, Dark Rosaleen, the Rose of Ireland . . . the stories of Ireland were peopled with sad, tragic figures, Cathleen ni Houlihan mourning the loss of her four beautiful green fields, demanding that young warriors give their lives for her . . .

He eased open the door of Cathal's room. The boy was asleep; his mouth was slightly open and his light-coloured hair was pushed back from his forehead; his face in repose looked very young. His eyelids did not flicker to the sound of Patrick's tread. Patrick put the envelope on the bedside table where Cathal would see it when he woke up, then removed a cup of cold tea and crept out of the room.

He went out to the garden with his drawing materials and before long was absorbed in his drawing, concentrating on the intricate foliage of the clematis which scrambled over Aunt Margaret's new pergola. He did not know how long he had been there when he heard the sound of hurried footsteps on gravel.

Startled, he looked up to see Michael MacBride rushing round the side of the house. The boy stopped dead as he saw Patrick sitting on the bench. He was panting as if he had run all the way from home.

"Are you the only one here?"

"Yes. Whatever's the matter?"

"It's Cathal," the boy blurted out. "He's gone to join the Rising – I tried to stop him, but I couldn't –"

Patrick stared at him. "But the Rising was cancelled, yesterday –"

"Yes, but it's on again today – Donal said so – at twelve o'clock –"

"And anyway Cathal's here. He's upstairs asleep in bed."

"He isn't. I've just seen him in the street, with a rifle –"

"Oh, Mother of God –" Patrick pushed past Michael and ran into the house and up the stairs three at a time. He couldn't believe what he had just heard, half-sure that he would see Cathal lying asleep as before. He pounded across the landing.

The room was empty. The bedclothes were flung back and Cathal's pyjamas were strewn across the floor. Patrick snatched up the empty envelope and raced back down the stairs, colliding with Michael at the bottom.

He thrust the envelope in the boy's face. "If Cathal knew about the change of plan it must be you who told him!"

Michael stepped back, his eyes dark and frightened in the gloomy hallway. "No! That was from Donal, not from me. He made Roisin bring it – she's only told me just."

"You mean – and I *gave* it to him . . ."

"Siobhan will murder me when she finds out – she told me –"

Patrick thought quickly. "Where will he have gone?"

"They start from Liberty Hall. But there might not have been time. If not he'd probably go straight to the Post Office. Donal's orders were to go there, with Pearse and Connolly."

"Oh God. There isn't a hope of finding him." Nevertheless Patrick was already on his way through to lock the back door.

"What will you do?"

"Go after him. How long ago did you see him, and where?"

"By the shop, about ten minutes ago by now."

"By himself?"

Michael nodded. "Donal's already gone on. He was going to try and catch up."

"Come on." Patrick pushed Michael ahead of him out of the front door and closed it. Then he was out in the street and running, quickly outpacing the younger boy. Jesus, what could he do? He didn't have a chance of finding Cathal with ten minutes' start . . . He was nearly at the junction with the main Rathmines Road. A small car was coming along slowly, going towards the city. Patrick, running for all he was worth, reached the junction just in time to leap wildly in front of it, waving his arms. The car skidded to a halt, and he lost his balance and all but collapsed on the bonnet. The elderly driver glowered at him in indignation.

"Is it mad you are?"

Patrick tried to look more normal. "Can you take me with you? It's desperate – I've got to find someone –"

The driver looked at him sternly for a moment and then, apparently deciding that he wasn't an armed vagabond, leaned across to open the passenger door and said, "Get in, young feller. I'll take you as far as the river."

Patrick hurled himself in and the driver let the clutch out and drove on with maddening slowness. As the car moved off, church bells rang out from the Catholic Church on the Rathmines Road. It was the twelve o'clock Angelus.

The driver paused to cross himself and to mutter a rapid prayer, and then the car proceeded on its dignified, painfully slow journey towards the city. Patrick, unsure whether it would be quicker to get out and run, sat in a frustrated agony of inaction, trying to look in every direction at once, scanning the pavements and street corners for any glimpse of Cathal.

"Sit tight, young feller," the driver said. "We'll get there in God's own time."

He sat hunched over the steering wheel, gripping it fiercely in leather-gloved hands as if the car were a frisky horse which might bolt off at any moment. If only it were, Patrick thought desperately, hardly able to contain his urge for frantic activity. Underneath lurked the dark hollow depth of his knowledge that he had failed, failed utterly. He had let Cathal give him the slip. Preventing it was the one important thing he had had to do, and he had failed. Worse, he had actually given Cathal the message which had sent him running out to join his heroes . . . He had let them all down, his aunt and uncle, Siobhan, Cathal, himself.

How would he ever find his cousin in a city full of people?

As the car crossed the canal bridge into Camden Street it occurred to him that it did not look much as if an armed uprising were in progress. The streets were dotted with people dressed in summery clothes, strolling along in family groups, enjoying the Bank Holiday sunshine. He was not sure what he had expected – a scene like the retreat from Mons, or the Gallipoli landings? But there was nothing at all in the calm summery streets to suggest that anything out of the ordinary was happening. Could there have been another mistake? In all the confusion, had Donal got it wrong? Why would the Rising be cancelled one day and planned again for the next? If it was a plan to deceive the authorities, surely it was just as likely to confuse the participants . . .

Then he saw, crossing the road ahead, a line of troops in Volunteer and Citizen Army uniform.

"There go the go-boys," the driver said. His tone was affectionate, as if he were speaking of a group of naughty schoolboys, Patrick thought. The man turned and looked at him with alert blue eyes. "Is it after joining them you are?"

"No," Patrick said. "I'm trying to stop my young cousin before he does."

"Sure, they never get enough of marching up and down. He'll likely enough come to no harm."

It was hopeless, getting ever more hopeless as the minutes passed and the car progressed on its unhurried way between the pavements lined with pedestrians. He would never find Cathal. Cathal could be in the Post Office by now, taking his place triumphantly. And what would happen then? Patrick knew that it must be only a matter of time before troops arrived to flush the rebels out, or gun them down. Thank God he was in an English regiment and not an Irish one . . . in different circumstances he could have been in uniform today, instructed to shoot at his own countrymen, his own cousin . . . He could not have done it. He would have had to refuse to obey orders.

"I'll put you down here," the elderly driver said. "Don't be getting yourself into trouble now."

"I won't. You're not going up Sackville Street are you?" he added, half out of the car. He did not want the old man to drive unwittingly into the fray, if there was one.

188

"I am not. I'm on my way to see my sister in Artane."

Patrick shouted his thanks as the car pulled away. Then, breaking into a run, he made for O'Connell Bridge, dodging and weaving through the crowds. It was clear by now that something was happening, something which was causing mild curiosity rather than excitement or panic; people gathered in knots on the bridge and by the O'Connell statue, looking up Sackville Street. O'Connell, Patrick remembered as he ran, had said *No amount of human liberty is worth the shedding of a single drop of human blood . . .* Nelson's pillar, flanked by the tall stately buildings on either side of the broad street, stood aloofly above. Patrick crossed the bridge and ran in the direction of the General Post Office. The massive granite building with its impressive facade was on the left; it was here that most of the crowds were gathering, looking on with interest or amusement. Gasping for breath, Patrick stopped and looked across at the pillared frontage. The doors were closed, and the glass had been smashed out from the windows, the spaces jammed up with wood, mailbags and what looked like typewriters. He was too late. The rebels had barricaded themselves inside.

Noticing that people were pointing up at the roof, Patrick looked up and saw that the Union Jack which usually fluttered there had been pulled down and that two new flags were flying in the mild breeze: one an orange, white and green tricolour and the second a harp on a field of green, with IRISH REPUBLIC painted underneath in gold.

He stood panting and wondering what to do now,

his stomach muscles protesting at the strenuous effort of running. Could he get inside the Post Office? There were rifle-butts protruding from the windows . . . he might be taken prisoner or even shot, and that would do nothing to help the situation. Even if he did succeed in getting in, would he be able to get Cathal out? But maybe Cathal had not got here in time . . . if he had walked or run from Rathmines, Patrick could have overtaken him in the car or passed him coming by a different route . . . Cathal could be here somewhere in the crowds, waiting for a chance to dash in . . .

While he weighed up the options, he took in fragments of conversation from the people around him.

" . . . Bloody Sinn Feiners . . . How am I to get my separation money?"

"My man's in the trenches fighting for the good of bowsies like these."

"Calling themselves the Republic of Ireland, that feller Pearse said. Did you ever hear the like?"

"Wait till the soldiers come and get after them. 'Twill be a different song they'll sing then."

The shoe-shine boys and flower-sellers who had been dislodged from the steps of the Post Office were complaining about the loss of trade, and the sound of smashing glass announced that other people were taking advantage of the situation to break into the shops and steal whatever they could find. These, Patrick remembered ironically as he scanned the crowds for the one face he wanted to see, were the ordinary people of Dublin who would rise up and support the rebels, according to

Pearse's confident prediction. From the remarks he overheard, it was clear that the people in Sackville Street were not seeing the spirit of Ireland rise above her oppressors to take her place among the nations of the world. What they were seeing was a gang of ruffians who were spoiling their Bank Holiday and stopping them from getting their separation money at the Post Office counters.

Patrick heard only one voice speak up in favour of the rebels. "Sure, and every true Irishman should be wearing the green today."

A phrase from the familiar song slipped into Patrick's mind:

She's the most distressful country that ever yet was seen;

They're hanging men and women there for the wearing of the green . . .

Hopelessly undecided, he knew only one thing: he couldn't go home without Cathal. He imagined himself telling his aunt and uncle and Mary, "I'm afraid Cathal's gone to join in the Rising. I know I was supposed to look after him, but I gave him the information about it and then sat in the garden while he ran off . . ." He could hardly believe that he was capable of such incredible, crass stupidity. But for that little piece of paper, he would have been sitting in the garden with nothing to worry about but the perspective of the roof-line in his drawing, and Cathal would have been asleep in his bed . . . But what was the point of going over it? He couldn't go back in time and tear the note up. It had happened, and Cathal was here somewhere, and something had to be done about it. He walked to and fro, looking at everyone in the crowd who vaguely resembled his cousin. He did not even know what Cathal would be wearing.

Amidst the pushing and jostling as more and more people joined in the looting, emerging from the broken shop windows with armfuls of clothes or bottles of whiskey, there was a new focus of interest. Some of the onlookers were gazing away from the Post Office, in the direction of the Parnell Monument further up Sackville Street. Horses' hooves rang on the metalled road.

"Lancers!" someone shouted.

"It's our boys, come to show them what real soldiers are like!"

As the crowd moved aside, the mounted riders came into view, a column of them, with red and white pennants fluttering from their lances. God, Patrick thought with a thrill of fear, what were they going to do? Mount a cavalry charge, as if this were the Crimea? He couldn't see what use it would be, with the rebels behind barred doors and windows . . .

The Lancers began to advance, moving smoothly into a trot. The sun glinted off shining bits and stirrups and the glossy coats of the horses; they were immaculately turned out in every detail. Patrick, retreating to the pavement, looked across the street at the first-floor of the Post Office and saw excited movement at the windows. He realised that the rebels were going to fire at the troops; the crowds, who had been getting bored waiting for something exciting to happen, were going to see action. Then his attention was caught by another surge of movement at the Post Office doors: Volunteers in uniform, late-comers, were trying to get in. They banged at the doors and windows, and some ran round to the sides of the building. Then a slim figure in civilian clothes, a rifle slung over one shoulder, detached itself from the crowd on Patrick's side of the street and ran across to join them.

Cathal …

The Lancers were level with Nelson's Pillar, moving at a brisk trot, their hooves sending sparks off the tram-rails. Patrick elbowed his way between the people in front of him and launched himself off the pavement in pursuit of Cathal. The horses were so close now that his senses registered the smell of their sweat, and the taut faces of the riders and the jingle of harness; the officer leading the column gave an exclamation of surprise as Patrick dived almost under his horse's nose. Cathal was just a few yards ahead, intent on getting into the building with the latecomers. Then the crack of rifle fire resounded from the upstairs window, swiftly followed by yells of encouragement and other volleys from both sides of the road. The rebels were firing wildly at the troops with more enthusiasm than marksmanship. There was a scream from someone in the crowd as a horse went down with wildly flailing hooves, and then a confusion of shouted commands, rifle fire and terrified neighing. Patrick took in all this without taking his eyes off Cathal. Then Cathal, distracted by the shooting and the confusion, glanced back and saw Patrick as he made a desperate lunge towards him. For a split second he was rooted to the spot with amazement, allowing Patrick to grab him by both arms.

"God Almighty, Cathal," he said into his ear, pinioning him more firmly.

"Let me go – let me *go* –" Cathal fought and struggled, almost weeping with frustration, but Patrick, far stronger, had him in a firm grip. He had done it, *he had done it* . . . And then something slammed into him from behind, tearing into his left shoulder and spinning him round, knocking the breath out of him. He thought at first that one of the horses had lashed out and caught him with a flailing hoof, but then realised that he had been shot . . . Jesus, had he come this far just to be shot down, to let Cathal give him the slip again . . . But somehow he was still clutching Cathal to him as he staggered, and he heard the boy's gasp of fear as the force of the impact knocked them both to the ground. Patrick recovered first, impelled by his determination not to let Cathal go. He rolled over, pain scorching through his shoulder, and pinned Cathal down between his knees. His head reeled, and he felt the trickle of blood down his shoulder blade, and his shirt sticking hotly to the wound. Cathal's pale tearful face was blurring in front of him. In a minute he would pass out, and Cathal would get away . . .

He looked up. The Lancers were retreating in disorder, leaving behind the glossy perfectly groomed mound of the dead horse, its flanks still gently steaming. And four riders, one of them just a few yards away . . . an upturned white face, and a slow trickle of blood from the mouth . . . someone screaming up at the windows, "You murthering swine, killing our darling soldiers . . . Is it madmen you are?"

Cathal turned his head and saw all this too. The Rising was no longer a plan in the heads of

dreamers, but reality. First blood had been drawn.
For a moment Patrick thought that Cathal was
beaten, but then he recovered and began struggling
with renewed strength, freeing his arms and swiping
at Patrick's face.

"Let me go! I hate you ! You won't stop me . . .
I'm going in – "

Patrick knew that he could not hold on much
longer. He felt sick with exhaustion and fear and
the pain of his wound. And then he saw ambulances
moving slowly down the street, and the onlookers
who had been immobilised at the side of the road
during the shooting were coming out to help.

"All right, all right, we've got him," a voice said
in his ear. Someone bent to take hold of Cathal,
and someone else had hold of Patrick's right arm
and was helping him to stand up. Yet somehow he
wasn't rising after all but sinking, sinking slowly
into the dark mind-blotting depths that had been
waiting for him.

Dublin Castle

Coming back to consciousness was like floating
slowly to the surface of a dark lake. Oddly assorted
visions loomed and swam before him in sharply-
perceived detail. Smooth sweep of coastline, blue-
green sea stained red, foaming and boiling . . .
A dead horse, its tongue lolling out, big eyes
staring . . . Bodies, floating khaki shapes plumed
with scarlet, rising and bobbing on the tide like dead
starfish . . . *Get down, dig in, take cover . . . It's
suicide to go out there . . . You murthering swine,
killing our darling soldiers* . . . a trickle of blood
on the road surface, glistening . . . And the dying
face, raised to the sky in a grimace of death, the
pale face sinking into the cloudy disturbed depths,
Brendan's face, the Lancer's, Edward's, Cathal's,
all dead . . .

Patrick realised, with detached curiosity, that
he was not dead. He was alive and breathing.
He opened his eyes and stared up at a glittering
chandelier hanging from a plaster ceiling with ornate
curlicued mouldings. He was lying in a bed between
clean sheets; raising his head slightly he saw that
his left shoulder and arm were swathed in bandages

and wrapped in a sling, the whole arm lifted above the bedclothes. He felt no pain, but sank back, confused. The faint swaying in his head told him that he was still on the hospital ship, but this ship had windows through which he had seen glimpses of a courtyard . . . He closed his eyes, and a nurse came to him and said cheerfully, "You're awake, then. How are you feeling?"

She had an Irish accent. He opened his eyes. "Where am I?"

"In the Castle."

"Sudd-el-Bahr?"

"What?" She frowned, not understanding what he had said. "In the Castle," she repeated. "In hospital. They had to operate to get the bullet out. Now you try and get some rest. The MO will come and see you in a while."

Dublin Castle. Bullet. He was in Dublin Castle. He was in one of the State Rooms which were being used by the Red Cross, not far from the spot where he had stood a few days ago looking in through the gates. And he remembered the rest as well, the dash into the city, the Lancers, grappling with Cathal . . . What had happened then? He remembered passing out, Cathal shouting "I hate you –" . . . for all he knew, Cathal could have broken away and joined the rebels after all . . . How could he find out?

The other men in the gallery were veterans of the Western Front. There had been shooting outside in the Castle courtyard, Patrick gathered from their conversation. Most seemed cynical about the Rising, but rumours were flying: The rebels held strongpoints all over town . . . the whole country was up in arms . . . British gunboats were

shelling the city . . . a German submarine was on
its way up the Liffey to support the rebels . . .
No-one seemed to know what was really happening,
beyond what had gone on in the immediate vicinity
of the Castle: a policeman had been shot dead
at the gate, and there had been fighting in the
Upper Court before rebels took over the City
Hall. But now there were soldiers armed with
machine-guns in the castle yards, and later in the
day marksmen had shot dead a Citizen Army officer
as he tried to unfurl a green flag on the roof of the
building. The man had died, someone said, with
the green flag furling itself like a shroud over his
body . . .

They're hanging men and women there
For the wearing of the green . . .

When another nurse appeared, Patrick called her
over and said, "I must get a message to my family
in Rathmines."

She shook her head. "There's not much chance
of that now. The city's under martial law. It's all
we can do to get the ambulances in here, with the
fighting going on."

There was nothing to do but lie and wait. He was
still affected by the anaesthetic, drifting in and out
of restless sleep. Snatches of conversation reached
him . . . "The Sinn Feiners are in Jacob's Biscuit
Factory." "They won't starve then – they can live on
lemon creams and chocolate wafers . . ."

A biscuit factory and a Post Office, Patrick
thought drowsily; they seemed unlikely as military
strongholds . . .

"Well, they've been in there for two days now and
the troops haven't shifted them . . ."

Two days. It was Wednesday, and he was supposed to be catching the mail boat. He was to go before the Medical Board on Friday. He spent some time worrying about this in a vague way before his dull mind registered that he couldn't possibly be passed fit for active service now that he was lying in a hospital bed with a raw bullet wound . . . But how would anybody know what had happened to him?

His shoulder, now that the anaesthetic had fully worn off, flared into a mass of pain. They gave him morphia, and he slipped into the familiar routine of floating away from his body, drifting back, sharply alert for a minute or two and then dreaming . . .

A face loomed in front of his eyes.

"Patrick. *Patrick*."

"What?" he murmured. Why wouldn't they let him sleep?

"Patrick, it's me, Siobhan. It's all right. Cathal's at home."

He tried to look at the blurred face but it was dissolving into dark wavering fragments, the voice fading into the distance. Some while later, he thought he remembered dreaming that someone had come and told him that Cathal was safe. He wanted to believe it, but it was just another of the voices in his head . . .

Later, when he was more normally awake, the nurse came over to him and said, "You had a visitor. You were half-asleep at the time, but she wanted to make sure you understood her message. Miss MacBride, one of our ambulance drivers. She said to make sure you know your cousin's safely at home, and she'll come back and see you as soon as she can."

Cathal safe at home . . . Patrick tried to feel relief. Perhaps there had been some point to getting himself shot after all, even though Cathal would not thank him for it, but hate him. The rebellion had already held out for longer than anyone could have expected, and he had denied Cathal his part in the death-or-glory enterprise . . .

By the time Siobhan returned, on Thursday evening, it was clear that the rebels were facing imminent defeat. The British were using a gunboat and artillery to shell the GPO and surrounding buildings. There were already fires in Sackville Street, she reported.

"It can only be a matter of time. They'll destroy the city to get a handful of men out. They could starve them out if they waited, but no, they have to go crashing in with the big guns."

Her face was drawn and pale. She must be desperately worried about her brother Donal, Patrick thought, for all that she knew he had taken the risks gladly.

"They are such fools," she burst out. Patrick, thinking she meant the British, realised his mistake when she continued, "Carrying on with the Rising after MacNeill put that notice in the papers. They must have known they'd reduce their chances by half . . ."

"What was it all about, the last-minute change?" Patrick asked.

Siobhan lowered her voice so that only Patrick could hear. "The ship bringing the German arms was discovered. It went down in Queenstown harbour. And the man who was arrested near Tralee last week was Sir Roger Casement, with a German railway ticket in his pocket. That's why MacNeill cancelled the plans – he hadn't wanted the Rising in the first place. But then the other leaders voted to go ahead. They knew it was their last chance before they were rounded up and arrested. I couldn't stop Donal. I didn't even know about it. I tried to make him keep Cathal out of it when I thought it was Sunday, and he promised me he would . . . and then on Sunday morning I thought everything was all right . . ."

She was near to tears with exhaustion and worry. Patrick wanted to comfort her, but could think of no comfort to offer. She broke off, closing her eyes, and then said, "I'm sorry. It's all my fault you're lying here now. Can you ever forgive me?"

"There's nothing to forgive. What happened would have happened whether you'd told me beforehand or not."

"Maybe you saved Cathal's life. But you could have got killed yourself."

"It was just a matter of chance."

"Stop trying to pretend that you weren't brave."

"I wasn't at all brave. There's more to bravery than getting in the way of a stray bullet. I just didn't think. Anyone would have done the same. You're far braver yourself, driving about the city in the thick of it." And never knowing whether the next casualty might turn out to be her own brother, he added silently.

"I'll come and see you again when I can. Do you mind?"

"Do you think I mind?"

Their eyes met, and then Siobhan smiled and said, "Is there anything I can do for you meanwhile?"

"Would you get someone to send a telegram

201

to my father? He'll have expected me at home yesterday."

She left to go back on ambulance duty, and Patrick watched her small figure dwarfed by the massive door of the gallery as she left. He wondered what news the next day would bring. He had no reason to feel any liking for Donal, but he hoped for Siobhan's sake that he would get out of the GPO safely.

There was nothing to do but wait it out, picking up what news he could from people coming in and out. What must it be like in the Post Office, he wondered, scorched by the heat of the nearby buildings, waiting for the artillery to score a direct hit? The roar and crash of the shelling could be heard in the Castle, and as it grew dark the sky above the city was orange with the glow of flames.

"Sure, they'll never be happy till they've burned down the whole of Dublin," someone said.

"German Zeppelins couldn't be worse than this."

"We mightn't be able to stay in here much longer."

Patrick, getting out of his bed to look at the limited view out of the window, was appalled. How could the scratch troops of the Volunteers and the Citizen Army, much derided by the regular soldiers, have provoked such a devastating response? Patrick remembered what Siobhan had said: a more effective, less destructive solution would have been to starve the rebels out. Was this terrible bombardment really the only way to dislodge them? Did they pose such a threat to the British Empire that it had to use tactics more suitable for the European War? It didn't make sense.

By Saturday evening, when Siobhan came again,

there was fresh news: Pearse had ordered a general surrender. The big guns had fallen silent. The Rising was over.

Ireland was still pink, Patrick thought.

Siobhan was white-faced and controlled, not tearful this time. "They'll be executed, Pearse and Connolly and the others who signed the Proclamation. They must have known that when they signed it."

"Connolly's here in the Castle. He was shot in the ankle."

"They'll execute him all the same," Siobhan said bleakly.

Patrick didn't tell her the other piece of news he had heard earlier in the day. General Maxwell, arriving in Dublin to put down the rebellion for once and for all, had ordered the digging of a huge pit at Arbour Hill Detention Centre, with mounds of quicklime ready. Big and deep enough for a hundred corpses, it was said.

Reprisals

"Well, if you're really sure," Aunt Margaret said. "You know we're all happy to have you here for as long as you wish. Well, apart from Cathal, I mean," she added truthfully.

"It's kind of you. I appreciate it," Patrick said. "But I think I really should go back home. Father's been expecting me, and you've put up with me for long enough."

On his return from hospital to the family house in Rathmines, he had found things rather difficult. Cathal, far from demonstrating the loving gratitude to Patrick which his mother and sister expected, refused even to speak to him. More than once, as he was about to enter a room, Patrick heard a fierce muttered conversation between Cathal and his mother or sister, abruptly broken off as he appeared on the scene. Cathal would usually march straight out of the room, head high, or bury his head in a book. And the family was divided in other ways besides, Mary denouncing the Rising as the work of madmen, Uncle James condemning the ferocity of the British reprisals: "They'd rather see Dublin reduced to a smouldering heap of rubble than let us have it for ourselves."

On Wednesday, when news was given out that Patrick Pearse had been executed by firing squad together with Clarke and MacDonagh, Cathal retreated into a bitter, stony-faced silence, speaking to no-one, as if his grief was too deep to be expressed in words or tears. Patrick thought he understood. Cathal had, after all, come more into contact with Pearse than any of the rest of them, and knew the force of his intense, mystical personality. Patrick wondered whether his cousin would understand his own admiration and grief for Pearse. There was more in common between Cathal and himself than Cathal would ever acknowledge. But there was no point in trying to explain.

Aunt Margaret tried to smooth over the awkwardness.

"I hate to think we're driving you away," she told Patrick. "I'm sorry about Cathal – he won't listen to any of us."

"He's bound to be upset," Patrick said, "with the news of the executions. And more to come."

"Yes. I can't help thinking it's a terrible mistake . . ."

Mary, hearing of Patrick's decision to leave, was upset. "It's because of Cathal you're going, isn't it?"

"No. There are other reasons. I shall come back, Mary. And I shan't forget your kindness."

He remembered that he had returned to Ireland to escape from war-weary London. Now he was returning to England from war-shattered Dublin.

"We'll never forget what you did for us," Mary said. "Cathal could have been killed but for you."

Patrick smiled, waggling his arm in its sling.

"Perhaps I should be grateful to him for this. Without it, I'd have been on my way to the Western Front in a week or two. Perhaps he's saved me from getting my head blown off. Who knows?"

Mary refused to be light-hearted. "Please don't talk like that, Patrick. I hate to think about it."

"Maybe it'll all be over by the time I get there. I seem to be good at leaving things too late."

Siobhan had promised to call and see him on his last evening. Waiting for her, he went out into the garden and stood looking back at the house, remembering the drawing which he still hadn't finished. The trees and shrubs were in full leaf, and his nostrils caught a drift of honeysuckle on the warm air. The dark foliage of Mary's clematis was splashed with pale mauve starry flowers. Patrick listened to a thrush singing from the rowan tree, and thought of the dead men who would not see spring turn into summer. Patrick and Willie Pearse, Thomas Clarke, Thomas MacDonagh, Joseph Plunkett, Edward Daly, Michael O'Hanrahan . . . the list was growing day by day. All of them lay in General Maxwell's quicklime pit. Maxwell, Patrick thought bitterly, knew better than to give the Irish more Fenian graves for martyrs' shrines.

He heard Mary's voice as she led Siobhan through the back door and brought her out to him. They greeted each other in subdued fashion; Siobhan was still waiting for news of Donal, who was held with other prisoners in Richmond Barracks.

"Have you heard anything today?" Mary asked.

Siobhan nodded. "Countess Markiewicz has been given life imprisonment, not the firing squad. Along with some others."

Patrick, who knew that Mary's private opinion was that shooting was too good for the rebels, thought that she would probably not extend this judgment to include Donal. She said, "I'll be thinking of you," and went back into the house, leaving Siobhan and Patrick to talk in private.

Siobhan was dressed in her unbecoming driver's uniform, the large brimmed hat making her face look small and delicate, even elfin. Her dark eyes were tired, shadowed underneath. Patrick remembered how vivacious she had appeared when they first met. It would take definite news of her brother's reprieve to bring back her characteristic vitality, he thought.

All the same, he thought she looked beautiful.

"I'm sorry to be going back to England without knowing about Donal," he said. "But the news today sounds promising. The authorities couldn't be such fools as to carry on once the leaders are dead . . . and public opinion is turning against the executions. Did you see the *Daily Chronicle?*"

"I did. I'll write to you as soon as I hear anything." She looked away. "They said at first that everyone over eighteen would have been executed. Thank God they saw sense . . . They'll execute the other signatories, though. Ceannt and Mac Diarmada and Connolly."

Patrick thought of James Connolly lying in a hospital bed in the Castle, suffering the agony of an ankle turning gangrenous. It was horrible, callous, he thought, to treat a man for his injuries with the aim of making him fit enough to take him out and shoot him . . . Patrick was appalled by the thought of the firing-squad. It was one thing to get shot at in the heat of the moment, quite another to stand there blindfolded and condemned, waiting for the bullets to tear into you, hoping for a quick and merciful end . . . Would you be sure, right up to the end, that your beliefs were worth dying for? Did dying *make* you believe so?

"Perhaps," he said, "for all of them, it's the death they would have chosen. To die a soldier's death for Ireland."

Since Wednesday, he had thought again and again of Pearse, the poet, dreamer and idealist, walking out to face the firing squad. For all his imaginings of how he would face up to the ordeal himself, he couldn't imagine Pearse facing death with anything other than quiet courage. No-one who had ever seen him or heard him speak could doubt that he was motivated by sincerely-held principles. He must have been horrified by the violence he had seen unleashed. And yet his own actions had indirectly brought it about. He had dreamed his noble dreams, and his dreams had become a nightmare of blood and killing and terror . . .

"I can't stop thinking about all those other deaths," Siobhan said. "All those people the English soldiers murdered in Upper King Street . . . people who hadn't signed a Proclamation or carried a weapon. And the Lancers – it seems after all that they weren't attacking the GPO, just going down the street from one place to another. All that killing."

They were walking slowly to the end of the garden. Patrick said, "It sounds as though you're as unsure as I am . . . whether it was all worth it. Whether it's achieved anything at all."

Siobhan said slowly, "A number of brave, sincere, intelligent men have thrown their lives away, and dozens of others have been killed with them. I support their principles, but not what they did. It's the wrong time. The people weren't behind them. Most Dublin people would be quite content to wait for Home Rule. You said yourself that you saw people jeering, more interested in stealing from the shops."

"Remember that girl we saw outside Bewley's," Patrick said. "The girl begging on the street, with two babies. She's probably half-starving. Can you blame people like that for taking their chance?"

"No. If you were starving, it would make no difference whether you starved in an Irish Republic or under British rule," Siobhan agreed. "As for what it's achieved, I suppose we won't know . . . not until after the war . . . the other war, that is . . ."

The war in Europe seemed to have faded into the background, Patrick thought, pushed off-stage in everyone's thoughts by the more dramatic events at close quarters. But it was still there.

"You'll soon be going back to your regiment," Siobhan said regretfully.

"It'll be a while yet. Not until the end of the summer, the MO thought."

"I'll write to you."

Patrick said, "And I'll write back."

"I'd like that."

"You said a while ago that you were hoping to go to London. Are you still going to do it?"

She looked at him steadily. "I said before, I support the Irish troops but not the war. The Rising hasn't changed that. I'm not after staying

209

at home and waiting, when there's something useful to be done."

"We could meet again when you're in London," he suggested.

"I might be in France."

"So might I be. We must try to meet wherever we are."

She nodded, and Patrick saw that she was blinking back tears. She said, "It's awful, saying goodbye," and then broke off as if she did not trust herself to say any more.

His own eyes were smarting as he moved a step closer and then hesitated. She looked up at him and he said, "Perhaps it needn't be goodbye. We must make sure it isn't." And then he embraced her, somewhat encumbered by his arm in its sling. She felt small and fragile in his arms, so that he felt an illogical desire to protect her, for all his knowledge that she had enough strength of her own.

Over the top of her head he saw Aunt Margaret coming round the corner of the house into the garden. She stopped in surprise, and then tactfully withdrew.

PART THREE

LONDON,
SEPTEMBER 1916

Edward

Patrick got off the bus and walked in the direction of the 3rd London General Hospital. News placards in the streets read SOMME BATTLE CONTINUES and FRESH FIGHTING AROUND THIEPVAL. Ambulances passed him in the street, and three convalescent patients, all on crutches, were swinging their way with practised dexterity through the hospital gates. A private walking by on the pavement, saluted Patrick, who was once again a British army officer in uniform. Second Lieutenant P. Leary, Epping Foresters, 4th Battalion.

Since the Somme offensive had broken out on July 1st, he had been convinced that Edward had been killed, after all his premonitions. The wrench and pull of it was familiar, the undertow of his fear.

When Edward's note had arrived – *"I am in hospital in Wandsworth with a head wound, not serious"* – it had seemed to speak with the voice of a person resurrected from the dead. Edward had survived the Somme. He had gone through it and come out with a minor wound. Patrick himself had survived Gallipoli. He was encouraged to think that they might possibly see it through, both of them, in spite of shells, grenades and sniper's bullets.

Inside, he asked for directions to Edward's ward and was shown the way. He walked up to the first floor, inhaling the familiar hospital smells of disinfectant and floor polish and soup. He felt that he had already seen too much of hospitals. At the end of the corridor, by the ward entrance, a young private soldier was waiting. He too looked up and saluted, and then as Patrick reached the door it was pushed opened from inside and a young woman came out to join the waiting soldier. She thanked Patrick as he held the door for her, and he formed the impression of a strong likeness between the two – brother and sister? – before going through to the ward to look along the row of beds for Edward.

He had been wondering what to expect, remembering Edward's nervous tension after the Loos fighting last year. This time, Edward had been through something even worse than that, by all accounts. Patrick, who had seen the casualty lists on the inside pages of the newspapers, whole columns of names in tiny print, knew that Edward was well out of it.

The ward was for surgical cases: rows of men with bandaged wounds or the stumps of amputated limbs. Patrick felt almost guilty at being so conspicuously fit and healthy, even though he had had his share of being laid up. There was a gramophone playing, but through the music Patrick could hear the intermittent groaning of a man who lay with his entire chest and abdomen wrapped in bandages.

He recognised Edward at the end of the ward,

in spite of the bandage which covered most of his black hair. He was sitting in an armchair by the side of his bed, dressed in blue convalescent uniform. A Thomas Hardy novel lay open on the bed, but Edward was staring vacantly out of the window, apparently so engrossed in his thoughts that he did not notice Patrick approaching.

"Edward?"

Edward's head swivelled round. "*Pat!*"

Patrick, much relieved as Edward stood up and greeted him with positive enthusiasm, saw that he looked well in control of himself, far more normal in fact than he had at their last meeting. His face was perhaps thinner and paler, but his blue eyes were clear and alert beneath the bandage. *Eyes in a half-drowned face, flicking open, seeing, coming back to life . . .*

"I was hoping you'd be able to breeze in. But why do we only ever meet in hospitals?" Edward said as they sat down.

Patrick grinned. "We both seem to have a knack for getting ourselves shot at. What happened to you?"

"Sheer carelessness. For once we had a Brigadier-General with us, and luckily for us he had a grain of common sense. Our orders were to go on with an advance which anyone could see was hopeless. He actually called it off. And then, like an idiot, I stuck my head up over a ravine just as we were going back to safety. It isn't serious. Just a nice cushy Blighty one."

"It sounds like a terrible show, the Somme. And the newspapers have been reporting it as a victory."

Edward said, "*One more such victory and we are lost. Do you remember that?*"

"Could I forget? Dr. Prowse and his Roman history."

The dusty classroom . . . motes of dust hanging in the air . . . Dr. Prowse in his bat-like gown, gesticulating at scrawled diagrams on the blackboard . . . himself as a small boy doodling in the margin of his book . . .

"Defeating the Romans at Asculum, 279 B.C.," Edward recited briskly. "Isn't it amazing how these useless pieces of information stick in your mind?"

"They do in yours. I was always useless at dates," Patrick corrected him. "Do you remember how Dr. Prowse was the only master who could put Collard in his place?"

"Yes. *Collard, you have the mental agility of a dead haddock.* And," Edward added more pointedly, "*Leary, I realise that your furtive artistic activity is possibly more interesting to you than the exploits of Pyrrhus, but could you do me the courtesy of attending nevertheless . . .* "

Patrick laughed. "I wonder what's happened to him now? He seemed so old, but I suppose he was only in his late thirties."

"Too old to enlist, anyway. But tell me about this bit of bother over in Dublin. I followed it in the papers as best I could. I was out near Béthune at the time."

Patrick told him his version of events.

When he had finished, Edward said, "So you were shot in the back by a rebel sniper? Wouldn't you have preferred to be on the other side?"

"I wasn't on any side."

"You could have been."

"You think I should have been in the GPO in Volunteer uniform? What would you have done if you'd been there?"

Edward considered for a moment and then said, "Well, if I were an Irishman, and if I weren't already in the army, I think I'd probably have been in there with them."

"Would you now," Patrick said.

Edward looked at him sharply. "Just think what it would be like if Germany had taken over England and imposed its own government. If we stormed a London post office and held it against the Germans for six days, we'd be applauded for bravery and given medals, wouldn't we? Well, England to Ireland is what the Germans are to England. A foreign power."

"Well, and don't I know that well enough, but –"

"And," Edward continued, in full flow, "why is it that the British government has such an infallible talent for doing the wrong thing in Ireland?"

"You mean the executions?"

"Yes. If they'd deliberately set out to fan the flames higher they could hardly have thought of anything better. If they'd simply kept the rebel leaders in prison they'd have been forgotten. Now Pearse and the others will be legendary heroes along with the likes of Robert Emmet and Wolfe Tone. Just what they would have wanted, I expect. And now they've hanged Casement as well. But it will have achieved one good thing."

"And what's that?" asked Patrick, who had been debating this point with himself since April without coming to any definite conclusion.

"Ireland won't be content with Home Rule now. It will have to be complete independence."

Patrick took this in. Edward never failed to surprise him.

He said, "I hope to God you're right. It's odd to think that of the two of us you seem to be the stronger Republican."

"In a way. Brendan took a lot of convincing before he'd realise that . . . But I see it as an outsider, without the complications you had to think about. What happened to the MacBride brother, the one who was in the GPO?"

"He's in prison in North Wales. Much to the relief of his family. They were afraid he'd be shot with the others."

Patrick remembered that there was something he had been meaning to ask Edward.

"What was that piece of good news you mentioned in your letter? I've been wondering about it."

"Ah yes." Edward's face showed a mixture of smugness and embarrassment. "Well, I . . . The thing is, Pat, I'm going to get married."

"What? Get *married*? When?"

"It's not that outrageous an idea, is it?" Edward said, amused at his reaction. "Lots of people do it. Quite normal people. It happens all the time. It might even happen to you one day."

"You mean to the girl you talked about before?"

"Well yes." Edward raised one eyebrow. "How many girls do you imagine I've been dallying with? I'm going to marry Alice. You've only just missed meeting her. She's just been in to see me with Jack, her twin brother."

Patrick recalled the pair he had seen at the entrance, the girl and the soldier. He retained a fleeting impression of the girl's serious face and a coil of soft brown hair.

"It's a pity I didn't get here a bit sooner. You could have introduced us. Well, congratulations, then. When is this going to happen? The wedding?"

He saw a look of doubt cross Edward's face.

"In the spring. I hope I haven't done the wrong thing."

"You mean you're wondering do you want to marry her after all?"

"Oh God no," Edward said quickly. "I want that more than anything. I mean, because of what might happen. I hate the thought of leaving her a widow. For more than purely selfish reasons," he added. "I didn't intend to ask her until after the war, but – well, I did."

Patrick considered the problem. "But the war could go on for years. You can't keep your life in suspension. And Alice must know the risks just as well as you do. She must think it's worth it."

He remembered saying much the same thing when Edward had first told him about Alice. He had no new insights or solutions to offer. But Edward nodded slowly, evidently wanting this reassurance.

"That's what I've been trying to tell myself. And . . . well, at times like these . . . as you must know . . . the big, impersonal things in life, your sense of duty, nationality, honour or whatever name you call it, tend to let you down with a crash . . . It seems that all you can do is pursue whatever happiness you can find in your personal life."

219

"Yes," Patrick said. He intended to. In his tunic pocket was the latest long letter from Siobhan, which he had received that morning and had read five times. She would be in London within the next week, just a few days too late to see him before he left for the front. He had thought of telling Edward about Siobhan, but now decided not to. Even though he and Siobhan had written to each other every week since he had left Dublin, he did not yet feel sure enough about the relationship.

"What about you?" Edward said. "What are you going to do now?"

"I'm going to Charing Cross directly from here. I've been on an artillery course for the last three weeks."

"You're going straight out to the front?"

"I am."

"Next time you get yourself shot, why don't you make it last a bit longer? You've had two tries now," Edward said lightly.

"I'm not planning on a third. And yourself – don't go rushing back too soon."

It was time to go. Patrick, superstitiously wondering when he would see Edward again, stood up and put his officer's cap back on.

"Well, Pat, and don't be after getting yourself into trobble now, me darlin' boy," Edward said.

Patrick grinned. Edward was hopeless at putting on accents. His attempt at Irish brogue came out sounding more like a southern American drawl.

"Have a jolly good rest yourself, old chap, and keep your head down when the whizz-bangs come over," he replied, in best Sandhurst.

It was no more accurate than Edward's try, but

the light tone of the parting served to contain the emotion which he was sure they both felt.

Patrick sat on the top deck of the bus to Charing Cross and looked out at the late afternoon sunshine which was already starting to look autumnal. London seemed drab, tired of war. The bus crossed the river, and he looked out at the dun-coloured waters flowing sluggishly towards Westminster, where Big Ben was sharply illuminated in the western sunlight. The glittering windows of the Houses of Parliament made him think of the unshakeable power which still reached out across the Irish Sea to govern his country.

Unshakeable? No, not quite.

Thou art not conquered yet, dear land . . .

He thought of what Edward had said, about the big things in life letting you down. It was true enough, he supposed, thinking of his own big let-downs: his certainty that he was about to take part in a modern-day Iliad at Gallipoli; his desire to see Ireland freed. And yet, he thought, Edward had got the rest wrong. It wasn't enough just to think of your own personal happiness. You had to have something more, something beyond yourself. Something to believe in.

He was not sure whether his actions suggested a belief in anything. He had stood as an onlooker through the latest episode in Ireland's long, tragic history. And now he was heading for the Western Front to fight for England. He could equally have pledged himself to fight Ireland's war. His inspiration could easily have come from Patrick Pearse rather than Rupert Brooke. They were both

221

idealists and dreamers, and they were both dead, Brooke on his Greek hillside, Pearse in a prison limepit. Both had died with their romanticised notions of blood and sacrifice intact.

It seemed like choosing death. He was going to choose life. A belief in life. Perhaps that was what Edward had meant.

He got off the bus at Trafalgar Square and walked along the Strand. Charing Cross station was thronged with troops waiting to leave; protracted farewells were taking place all round. The station interior was gloomy, deeply-shadowed, dominated by khaki. Patrick made his way through to find his train.

Beneath the archway sat a flower-seller surrounded by baskets of chrysathemums: golden and bronze, fire-coloured chrysanthemums, a blaze of brilliant glowing colour. Patrick stopped for a moment, dazzled, and then walked on to the platform where the troop-train waited in a haze of steam.